Pieces of Madness

By Kasey Pierce

Edited by Leah Lederman

SOURCE POINT PRESS

Published by Source Point Press.
Printed in Taiwan by KrakenPrint.
Copyright © 2017 Kasey Pierce

ISBN-10: 1-945940-06-9
ISBN-13: 978-1-945940-06-4
Cover art by Ryan Lee
Design and layout by Joshua Werner

DEDICATION

To my con-family. You know who you are.

Also to those who've been with me on my journey from blogger to author. It's been a strange but fun ride. I'm glad you could join me and I wanted to let you know that it's far from over…

I'm just getting started.

CONTENTS

FOREWORD

"MADNESS."

For a guy who's seen as fairly sane by most people, I probably spend way too much time thinking about this concept.

Madness.

Insanity.

What separates the "sane" from the "wackadoodles."

Is it social norms?

After all, as the as the great Charles Addams once beautiful summarized, "Normal is an illusion. What is normal for the spider is chaos for the fly."

Does this make sanity a matter of perspective?

I watched a video online the other day made by a very passionate person who exercised great restraint in explaining, as calmly as possible, that dinosaurs are not real, were never real, and are all part of a conspiracy concocted by paleontologists desperate to keep their jobs.

Many people I know called this person crazy... but could "madness" sometimes be as simple of a matter as adamantly believing something that most others don't believe?

Is madness even combatable with evidence?

It wasn't too long ago that you would have been told you were insane – "mad" – if you suggested the Earth revolved around the sun... and, yet a recent study by the National Science Foundation found that, when asked, 25% of Americans stated that the sun revolved around the Earth.

Are they "mad" for believing this, or just wrong?

Could "madness" be rooted in different beliefs?

Is it "madness" to misjudge a trusted peer's intentions... or to guess incorrectly when confronted by the devil... or even to skin someone alive and carry their separated flesh around in your arms like a trophy?

I'd like to think I know the answers to these questions... but then I read a book like this and I start obsessing on the same question all over again:

"What is madness?"

I don't think there's any one easy answer to the question... but you'll get a glimpse at some of the pieces here, courtesy of Kasey Pierce.

I'd tell you to enjoy the journey, but were you to enjoy it too much...well...

Heh.

To do so might cause you – and others – to begin obsessing on madness a little too much, too.

Instead, I encourage you to experience these cerebral, chilling, and unsettling stories, all the while asking yourself if normalcy really is a matter of perspective, whether or not what you believe to be true is indeed just that, and how far from – or perhaps even close to – madness you may be.

"Madness."

It's always closer than you think.

Your friend in comics,
Dirk Manning

September 2016

Dirk Manning is the writer for such maddening comics as TALES OF MR. RHEE, LOVE STORIES (TO DIE FOR), and NIGHTMARE WORLD (Devil's Due Entertainment) and more. When not exploring the topic of madness in the graphic novel medium, he chooses to use his powers for good via WRITE OR WRONG: A WRITER'S GUIDE TO CREATING COMICS (Caliber). Dirk Manning splits his time between his writing desk, the seemingly-never-ending comic convention circuit, and the Internet. More than you probably ever wanted to know about Dirk (and his own special strain of madness) can be found online at www.DirkManning.com as well as on most social media platforms (including Facebook, Twitter, Instagram, etc) @DirkManning. Cthulhu is his homeboy.

LUKE

"Can you invite other-dimensional beings into your waking life?"

[Recorded June 12, 2014]

For the past twenty-three years, I've been asking myself that question, among others like it. I'm still trying to make peace with what happened. Before I can do that, though, I have to question whether it really happened at all. For twenty-three years, I've all been looking for the answers, the real truth to what happened. I wouldn't blame you for not believing. But this isn't for you. This is for me.

This is my truth. The truth I know.

It was June 12, 1991 and my mother was only four weeks from her due date. After eight years of being an only child, I guess Mom and Dad thought it was time. The idea of a little brother fascinated me; someone who would always be there with me. I mean, Amanda had

1

been my best friend since kindergarten but with her dad's job, there was always the threat of her moving away.

She seemed just as excited as I was to know it was a boy. We were as thick as thieves, but we longed to be sisters — in our innocent minds, it seemed pretty logical that she would marry him. We would even draw pictures of what they would look like on their wedding day. Small brown swirls on white construction paper, like my father's hair, along with two green dots for his eyes. That was my little brother. They had just settled on a name, too. Luke.

It was an exciting time.

That was the day my mother went into labor. Hearing the screams, Amanda and I dropped our crayons and ran for the kitchen. We stopped at the doorway to find my mother grasping onto her stomach in a sweat, dialing for an ambulance. Of course, my father had been called in early at the plant. Confused, I began to cry from sheer terror as I watched her. Amanda quickly wrapped her arms around me and assured me that it was going to be okay.

Amanda's mother, hearing the commotion from next door, darted through the screen door and into the kitchen. Instinctively, she took my mother's hand and helped orchestrate her breathing. A few minutes later the ambulance arrived and took her into their care. I rushed towards the stretcher but before I could reach her, Amanda's mother had snatched me up. She held me tight as I scrambled and clawed in an attempt to get away, and she told me we'd see my mom again soon.

I remember watching the ambulance roll away. I stopped kicking and collapsed into her arms, crying hard tears. She scooped me up and started for the house, taking me past Amanda who'd been watching from the porch. Amanda whispered to me, "Don't worry, Kristy.

He'll be here soon."

Thirty minutes later, we found ourselves waiting in a room with teal couches and tables filled with magazines. Amanda kept going on about her future husband but all I wanted was to see my mom. I was on the verge of crying again when my dad rushed through the door in his oil-splattered work attire. I ran towards him and he stretched out his arms to grab me.

With me planted on his hip, he made his way to the nurse's station and asked to see his wife. They gave him a room number and he quickly knelt down to let me go, "Now you sit tight and be a good girl." I protested, of course, but he said he had to go help Mom by himself. He said he would be right back for me. Then he hurried through the double doors.

It wasn't long after that, maybe another twenty minutes later, when a man in olive scrubs and surgeon's cap walked solemnly through the door. He removed his hat and Amanda's mother stood with her hand to her mouth. We stared up at him. It was as if it was all pantomimed; I don't remember hearing a sound.

Amanda's future love, my brother...Luke. He didn't make it.

The grief turned my parents into hollow people. Although I knew they still loved me very much, they seemed miles away. Over the course of the next few months, with them gone to a land of misery, I found more of a home at Amanda's.

Really, the tragedy brought us even closer. She, of course, did grieving of her own. At the time she figured that my baby brother was the only boy she was ever destined to be with. Her first broken heart by someone she'd never met and my heart broke for her. Many times I'd find her sulking in her tree house after school. For about two months, I knew I'd always find her there. It was a crisp October afternoon when that all seemed to change.

As I climbed the rickety ladder, I heard her speaking to someone. Her tone was giddy and light. I worried that she'd found a new playmate. When I reached the top and leaned forward into the treehouse, she was laughing and carrying on as she poured imaginary tea from a pot into a cup and saucer. I watched for a few moments, unnoticed. It was clear there was no one in the chair across from her.

Feeling my presence, she spun around, and I remember her saying, "Hey! I'm so happy you came over!"

"What are you playing?"

"Luke and I were having some tea. Would you like some?"

I stood for a moment before asking, "Luke? My...brother?"

She looked up from pouring her imaginary refill, nodding excitedly, "Yes! He's here!"

I reminded her that she knew perfectly well that my brother had died, then took a seat in the miniature wooden chair as she explained herself: "Just because we don't see something doesn't mean it's not real. God is real and He's invisible. Santa is always working on toys and has his cousin go to the mall to see us. So we never see him either. I know Luke's real, Kristy! I just know!"

I couldn't argue with that logic, at the time, and I'm not sure I wanted to. It would make Mom and Dad happy to know that he was still alive, I thought. I can still remember the looks on their faces when I ran into the living room to tell them the exciting theory. My mother's eyes welled up and my father just hung his head.

I was so confused. In that moment, I felt as if I had won the lottery only to find out it was a joke ticket. I had just wanted to make them happy. Dad asked me why I would want to upset my mother like that, and his question brought me to tears. Mom reached out to hold me. She knew my intentions were true. I climbed in her lap and told her I was sorry.

And I decided never to mention Luke to them again.

From then on, however, Amanda and I played with Luke quite a bit. He'd even come to school with us. Amanda would have her arm extended when we walked, as though they were hand and hand. Hopscotch, tea parties, and weekend sleepovers, Luke was always with us. However, it wasn't long before other kids started to notice our strange manner. They took note of us laughing and talking whilst facing the same direction...facing nothing. The empty space between us when we played "Ring around the Rosie" looked odd, I'm sure.

On the way home from school one day, I was walking alongside Amanda as she linked arms with the wind. In the distance, I saw James Mallerd, fellow classmate and all-around prick. His family had just moved to our town two weeks prior, and bullying was his MO since day one in our school. Stocky, but still standing few inches over everyone in the class, he struck fear into all of us. Seeing the jet black hair and pale skin coming our way, I knew Amanda and I were about to fall victim.

For a moment it almost seemed as if we were in the clear. We were nearly past him when he grabbed Amanda by her extended arm and nearly jerked it out of socket, "What's up, weirdo?! Playin' with your imaginary buddy, again?"

She struggled and whined as I hit his arm repeatedly to let her go. He shoved me to the cement, and I fell back hard, skinning my elbows. As she cried for him to release her, he just kept laughing and mocking her.

And then the unimaginable took place. He abruptly released her, threw his head back, and began to dig at his neck. Amanda immediately reached down to help me up, and then we both watched noticed James and his struggle. Gasping for air, he clawed at his collar. His face turned shades of red as his claw marks became a mess of blood and sweat. We stood there, frozen. We had no idea what we were witnessing.

James thrashed his head about violently and crashed to his knees, his face bloated and vein-ridden and turning purple. His neck looked like it was painted in fresh red brush strokes. He just kept on scratching at his flesh and gasping. Finally, his blood-soaked hands dropped to his side and his torso slumped. His weight took him forward so that he collapsed face first onto the cement, cracking his skull. Twenty-three years later, I still hear that sound when I think back. It wasn't seconds before a river of thick crimson oozed onto the cement from beneath the impact.

There was a brief moment of silence and birds chirping before we began to sob collectively and uncontrollably. We'd just watched a boy violently murder himself. At least, that's what it looked like. That's the only instant deduction our young minds could make. Hell, age aside, what the fuck would you call it?

Amanda turned to me with sudden urgency. She said, "We have to go. We have to go now!"

Being young, clueless, and stunned, that made sense. So we ran the three blocks all the way to her house. There was something I noticed amongst all the tearful chaos, though. Running beside Amanda, I saw her arm was extended behind her, and she was making a fist.

...He was still with us.

Talk radio blared at her house. Her father's three o'clock political program was on. Sneaking past undetected, we hurried up the treehouse ladder. We stood there in the treehouse and caught our breath. Finally, I broke the silence by asking aloud, "What…was that?!"

Still choking back tears, Amanda just shook her head. There were no words. That is, until we heard the sirens in the distance.

Someone had found James.

We shot each other a look of terror. In that moment, I found it instinct to grab Amanda's shoulders to say, "Don't. Say. Anything." She bit her lip and nodded in agreement. It's not that we were responsible. Yet, somehow, uncertainty about that lingered. We wanted no more part in the events that had just occurred. One thing we were sure of, though: we had both witnessed the same thing. That weighted secret became a padlock that hung from our necks. I still carry it to this day.

Hearing the distant commotion, I knew my mother would wonder where I was. I hugged Amanda and turned to leave. Silently, she pointed out my freshly scabbed elbows. "It was that backward hopscotch. I'm not too good at it, remember?" She narrowed her eyes and stared at me for a moment before giving me a firm nod. I nodded back.

We were now in on something that was bigger than ourselves. Little did we know just what it was. Little did we know that this was just the beginning. Mom bought the hopscotch story. It went along with the bloodshot and cried-out eyes. She took me into the bathroom to clean my wounds over the sink. I climbed on my knees atop the toilet and reached my arm over. Just as she turned on the water, we were both startled by the front door slamming shut, followed by the turning of deadbolts. My dad appeared, shaken, in the doorway.

"Miriam, I need you."

He looked at me gently and told me to stay put as she followed him to the living room. I climbed off the toilet and tiptoed to the doorway to listen. Some I couldn't make out, but what I did sent shockwaves through my small body.

"The Mallerd boy was killed three blocks over."

I remember the sound of my mother gasping, and I heard my dad moving actively around, checking windows and locking doors.

When I heard my mother's steps, I swiftly resumed my original position. She tried to maintain her composure, assuming I hadn't heard what was said. Turning the faucet on, she instructed me to lean in as she reached into the cabinet for the iodine. I asked quietly what Dad wanted. She drew a heavy, shaking sigh before calmly explaining, "Something happened to your classmate today — James. I don't know what. But we have to stay inside tonight, okay?" I simply nodded, prepared to follow suit with whatever she said.

We ate dinner in an unsettling silence. I could tell Mom and Dad really wanted to discuss what happened, but minus my presence. Practically force feeding myself, I finished quickly and asked to be excused to brush my teeth. My mother still followed her ritual of tucking me into bed and kissing my forehead. She turned on my nightlight and closed the bedroom door.

I waited a few moments until I knew she was a good distance down the hall then crawled over to my window to see if Amanda was in bed yet. Her room was directly across from mine, and we often exchanged silly faces at bedtime. I knew there wouldn't be any goofing around that night, though. I stared at her window and waited.

Just as my eyes became heavy and I was prepared to give up, the curtains parted and Amanda appeared wearing a bright yellow nightgown. She let out a half-hearted smile and waved. I waved back, feeling happy and reassured to see her. Before I could mouth "goodnight," she looked to her immediate left and began speaking. She wasn't talking to me.

I stared inquisitively as she looked back at me. She then raised her left arm to her side, perfectly aligned with her shoulder. Still looking at me, she smiled and slumped her head to the left, like she was leaning on someone's shoulder. It wasn't long before it hit me.

Luke was sleeping over with her.

I waved once more at her and at the empty space beside her before scooting back onto my bed. It seemed like hours before my body and mind finally gave in to slumber.

The next morning, James Mallerd was all over the news. I walked down the hall to find my mom and dad glued to the television in the living room. They were so intent on what they were watching that it took a moment for my dad to notice I was there. He motioned me over. Once I was within reach, he grabbed me up into his arms and held me tight. He clutched onto me as if I were his last possession. "I love you, sweetheart," he whispered. "Please be careful at school today."

"I'm taking you to school today, Kristy," my mother added. "You're not walking home and neither is Amanda. Her mother and I will both be there to pick you up." I nodded in agreement as my father set me back down.

My mother and I were both silent on the way to school. We simply exchanged smiles although she looked as if she longed to say something. I was unbuckling my seatbelt when she grabbed me towards her in a crushing embrace. She held me for a few moments then pushed my shoulders back to look me square in the face. "I love you so much, Kristy. You be safe today, okay?" I smiled as she kissed my forehead, then hopped out of the car.

Amanda was standing on the curb, waving goodbye to her mom. I ran to hug her, and I remember she whispered, "We're okay, Kristy...Luke wouldn't let anything happen to us."

I slowly pulled away and looking into her eyes. She was glowing with delight, and I was puzzled. I just couldn't think of how to respond. Shrugging off my questioning look, she smiled and took my hand on our way to class.

There was a lot more buzzing amongst the students in the classroom than usual. That came to a halt when our teacher, Miss Clarence, and our principal, Mr. Phillips, entered the room. There was no need to bring about calm. A hush fell over us the moment he stepped in.

"Alright," he said, "we all know what happened but we don't know why. This is a hard time for the school and for the Mallerd family..." We sat in a silence that spoke volumes as he continued. We clearly understood. After he left, the class stood as normal to say the pledge of allegiance.

When recess came, Amanda and I started for our usual spot just passed the steel benches. We sat in the grass together every day; there was always room for Luke in our circle. In an attempt to return to normalcy, we went on speaking with him. We asked his opinion on the wedding colors Amanda had picked out, and what they should feed the guests. By the end of recess, we'd established that pink and purple would be their theme colors and they'd serve lasagna with a side of M&M's at their reception. We giggled all the way back to class.

I think it was refreshing to Miss Clarence that we were carrying on so well after tragedy struck our community, and so close to home. I'm sure she took it as a triumph of the human spirit. In reality, she had no idea about Luke or the events that had transpired the previous day. To be fair, I'm not so sure I really did, either.

After school, I climbed into mom's Bonneville. She laughed when she greeted me. It was nice to see her smile again, though I had to ask what was so funny. Then she told me I was just a funny little girl. I smiled and shrugged before reaching for my seatbelt. As we started down the road, I asked her why I was so funny.

She cocked her head, smiled, and narrowed her eyes, "Oh like you don't know, silly goose. The way you gave your teddy a face."

I sat in silence figuring eventually I'd remember what she was talking about, but when we pulled into the drive, I still hadn't figured it out. Anxious and tired from last night, I trudged in and dropped my backpack to the floor. "Nuh uh, missy," my mother said. "You know your book bag goes in your room."

Rolling my eyes, I dragged it across the living room floor and down the hall. At my doorway, I saw something that made my heart stop. Upon my bed sat my teddy bear. My teddy bear, with construction paper taped to it…with brown swirls and two green dots.

My teddy wore Luke's face.

I strived to reason how this could have happened. Maybe I had done this and forgotten? Maybe Amanda had done it… I knew neither of those made sense, though. My thoughts were interrupted when I heard my mom call for me to wash my hands and prep for dinner. Still staring, I backed a few paces into the hall. I was silent as I went to wash up, struggling to rationalize what I had just seen.

Come bedtime, I slowly strolled to my bed and to the bear with Luke's face. He sat in the ray of moonlight that seeped through the window. I stared at him in bewilderment. My mother's sudden tap at the door startled me out of the moment. She asked if I had brushed my teeth then let out a slight chuckle at the bear. After calling me a goofball, she pulled back the sheets and I crawled into bed. I lay down next to the stuffed bear with a boy's Crayola face. My mother kissed my forehead before switching the night light on and shutting the door. Then it was just the bear and me.

Luke and I.

Even in the dark, the green dots pierced through me. The uncertainty of how this happened and the sudden fear of being left alone sent a jolt into my chest. I ripped the cardboard from my teddy, crumpled It, and threw it to the floor. That seemed to bring enough relief to my heightened anxiety that I was able to fall into a peaceful sleep, bringing an end to the unsettling event. Or so I thought.

The next morning, I awoke to find my teddy next to me and of course, the ball of construction paper on the floor. I climbed out of bed and went for the paper so I could throw it in my wastebasket. I was bending over to scoop it up when I noticed colors I hadn't used in the original drawing. In fact, it looked like a soaked red rag. Carefully, I started to unrumple it but screamed and threw it away from me before I could even finish. It was a mess of coagulated blood. I fell back onto the wood floor and scooted myself up to the bed away from it.

My mother ran in to see what the matter was. Seeing me on the floor next to a blood-soaked crumpled piece of construction paper, she grabbed up the paper, looked at me, then looked at the bear. Surprisingly, she smiled. She simply dismissed this strange happening on breaking my elbow scabs open in the middle of the night. Examining the bed, she asked if I got any on the sheets.

I remained silent. I could hardly move. Not finding

any more bloodstains, my mom told me to shower and put some more iodine on my wounds before breakfast. With that, she left the room casually. I sat there paralyzed for a few moments more.

At school, I made my way in to find Amanda. Spotting me in the hall, she waved, and then picked up the pace as she started towards me, all smiles. She hugged me and asked if she had completed the right problems for today's math class. I remember how cheerfully she asked her next question, "How was your sleepover?" I remember the chill of shock from those words, I didn't say a thing. In my mind, I was trying to make sure I heard her correctly.

Amanda dropped her backpack and took out a piece of folded, lined paper. She opened it and handed it to me. I took it from her slowly and read the words written on it in bold black crayon, "Staying with my sis. See you soon."

She was smiling until she saw my stony look. I suspected she'd been playing a cruel joke on me. I lowered my brows and clenched my fists in anger, grasping the paper tightly. She asked me what was wrong.

"You did this. You made this. And you gave my teddy a face."

Amanda shook her head feverishly. "No, I found this on my bed when I got home from school yesterday. Honest! I would never lie to you, Kristy!"

I looked at her sadly. Somehow, I knew she was telling the truth. She had to have been. Not only was it impossible for her to have snuck in my room and defaced my bear, but we never lied to each other. Ever. Knowing she was telling the truth, though…that made it so much worse.

I asked why this didn't scare her, but she simply said, "Why would it?" Before I could respond, the teacher called for everyone in the halls to hurry along to class.

Recess came and I was still lost in my puzzled thoughts. Still, Amanda and I met at our usual spot. We were sitting in the grass when she turned to say something to the absent space between us. Before she could though, I told her to stop.

She stopped her sentence and looked at me funny, "What's with you, Kristy?"

"He isn't real, Amanda. Dead things don't come back just 'cos we want them to. We need to stop."

Her confused innocent eyes welled up with tears, "He is real, Kristy! He's real, and you're hurting his feelings!"

When I told her that she needed to stop pretending and we needed to play a different game, she stood up and began to yell at me. Miss Clarence ran over to us, asking just what was going on. I'll never forget Amanda's response. Whipping around to face Miss Clarence, she shrieked, "She's hurting Luke's feelings!"

Miss Clarence looked puzzled. She asked just who in the world Luke was. Amanda pointed to the grass beside her, and I just hung my head as our teacher realized that all along, Amanda and I had secluded ourselves every recess to talk to an imaginary friend. Finally, she chuckled and said, "Oh honey, it's just pretend. Don't get upset."

This was the wrong thing to say. Filled with rage, Amanda ran forward and kicked Miss Clarence in the knee, calling her a bitch. I looked at my friend, who was still heaving with anger. At least I thought it was her. Now I wasn't so sure. I'd never even heard Amanda say "crap." Who was this calling our teacher a bitch—and kicking her?

Another teacher on the playground ran over and grabbed Amanda by her arm, dragging her off to the

Principal's office. Amanda called after Luke and I. When she was gone, the other children stared at me in silence. Miss Clarence, brushing off her polyester skirt, murmured, "Let's get you inside, too. I'd like to ask a few questions about this 'friend' you two have."

I took her hand and walked with my head hung low. Feeling the weight of my classmates' stares, I just wanted to disappear. As we made our way down the silent halls, Miss Clarence asked if Amanda had been behaving normally lately. I simply looked up to her shamefully and shook my head "no."

She opened the door to the office, where I saw Amanda pouting in a chair across from a stone-faced Principal Phillips. I took a seat next to my friend as Miss Clarence crossed her arms and stared at her. She was waiting for an apology. "Amanda! Tell Miss Clarence you're sorry!" Principal Phillips said. Amanda ignored the two adults, looking at me instead, "YOU need to apologize to LUKE!"

Miss Clarence rolled her eyes and Mr. Phillips threw up his hands. I told her to stop it right now and that this was just a game.

"No, he IS real!"

It was clear Mr. Phillips had just about enough of this by the way he slammed his hands on the desk. He informed Amanda that he was calling her parents. I was excused back to class. I gave Amanda one last look before leaving. She wouldn't look at me.

I didn't see her the rest of the day.

When my mother came to pick me up, it was apparent she'd been filled in. She had questions about Amanda. I simply dismissed it as a game that Amanda had ruined. There was a brief pause before she drew a sigh and asked, "Where did you get the name?"

I just looked at her sheepishly. I didn't have to say

anything. She closed her eyes and swallowed hard. Needless to say, it was a quiet ride.

That night, I checked for Amanda at the window, but she never showed. The next morning, I overheard my parents talking about Amanda going to see a specialist. Her parents had decided to pull her from school for psychiatric evaluation. It was weird not having her there but at the same time, I remembered feeling a bit of relief. I hadn't realized how abnormally we were acting until things got—well, back to normal. At recess, some of the girls even let me play hopscotch with them.

I did miss Amanda. I just didn't miss Luke.

When I got home, I wanted to check on Amanda. I shrugged on my coat and started to walk to the door when my father stopped me. He advised me to keep my distance from her for a while. She was going through a difficult time that he didn't want me to have anything to do with. That made me sad inside. I still loved her.

I crawled to the window to check for her that night, and she startled me. There she was, waiting for me, staring steadfast at my window. Her expression was stern and it burned right through me.

To break the intensity, I smirked and waved. She just closed her eyes and looked away. It was clear that my position on Luke had offended her deeply. I just wanted to make her laugh again. Then I had an idea. Running to my nightstand, I pulled out construction paper and a few crayons. I drew a picture of Luke with his tongue sticking out, then ran back to the window and waved frantically as to catch her attention. When she looked up, I held the picture up to the window. She didn't laugh, or even smile; her response was slightly peculiar. She squinted, gave me a thumbs-up, and left the window.

I sat confused for a moment. That is, until I turned the paper to face me. In place of the face I drew, there were words: "Meet me in the treehouse."

I shook with terror. I knew I hadn't written that. But who had? Who was meeting Amanda?

Fearing for her life, I opened the window and climbed out. As soon as my feet touched the grass, I started running to the treehouse. I still remember the cold dampness under my feet and the small pebbles that dug into them.

Amanda was halfway up the ladder already. I whispered harshly for her to wait but she couldn't hear me. When I reached the top of the ladder, she helped me in and gave me a hug.

"No, no—Amanda, I didn't write that note—"

She looked puzzled then just laughed, telling me to stop playing around. I tried to explain what had happened, but before I could, he appeared.

Out of the dark shadows of the treehouse stepped a boy our age with brown curly hair and green eyes. He wore pajamas as if he too had snuck from his house to meet us. Smiling, he said, "Hello" and opened his arms to us.

We stood there, stunned. And then the excitement set in. Amanda said, "Luke! I knew you were real!" We scurried across the treehouse and fell into his embrace. He was real! The three of us hugged and rocked for a few moments.

I became a little too warm, though, and started to pull away a bit. His grip tightened. Then he began to squeeze us both. Amanda must have been thinking the same thing, because I felt her try to pull away from this suddenly gridlocked group hug. We both whimpered as we tried to pull away, feeling uncomfortably hot now. I looked over his shoulder just then, and what I saw is what became the reoccurring vision in my nightmares. A constant reminder of what happened.

The wooden wall of the treehouse was no longer there. Instead were clouds of steam that cleared every half second to reveal a rocky, spiraling pit. Out of it came the moans and cries of people in immense pain. Screams that spoke of indescribable torture. Amanda and I screamed and thrashed about, but Luke only squeezed tighter. We were silenced when we looked up and saw his face.

His green eyes had been replaced with empty black sockets that looked straight into me while clots of blood poured from his mouth. The blood gargled as he spoke in a demonic tone that shook my chest, "Now you see that it's real...and it will be for an eternity."

He laughed horribly while we tried to shake loose of his grip. I managed to duck down and jerk from his arm, breaking free. I started to run but stopped, just out of reach, and looked back. Amanda was still in his arms. She looked to me helplessly and reached for my hand.

"I'm sorry, Amanda."

She was still reaching for me and she started screaming when I darted for the opening of the treehouse. I climbed down the ladder at lightning speed and only reached half way down before I jumped to the ground.

I could still hear her screaming; I could still hear the moans; I still heard the demon's laughter...but I didn't turn around until I reached my window. I looked back to see nothing but a dark tree house. Then there was silence.

I climbed back through my window, shut it, locked it, and shook as I hid under the covers.

That was the last anyone'd seen of Amanda.

So, now you know. You know the truth. Whether

you believe it or not is up to you. All the protection spells and prayers in the book have kept me safe but nothing can ever erase the memories. I escaped, but I still reside in Hell.

For twenty-three years she's burned. For twenty-three years I've kept silent. And for twenty-three years, I've wanted to die.

I'm sorry.

[End Tape]

Parapsychologist Dr. Kristine O'Brien was found dead Saturday morning at Johnson University. It appears she suffered a fatal gunshot wound to the head. Coroners have ruled it a suicide. She was thirty-one years old.

BESTIA

"Mr. Malcolm, do you think these nightmares may simply be a manifestation of your insecurities?"

Two months of therapy. Tom Malcolm had endured two months of therapy to free him from this insomniac prison. Going from a physical cell to a mental one seemed ironic for this ex-con— here he'd thought he'd be rewarded in his struggle for redemption.

Everyone makes mistakes. Attempted manslaughter wouldn't be your first guess, to look at him. Even members of the jury thought the sentence was a little steep. However, he did smack that biker's head against the bar floor a few times. The victim damn near bled out that night.

Tom had been in and out of foster homes since he came into this world. Born broken, you might say. In this world of "you get what you give," he gave what he got: hate.

That, and loneliness.

Now two years out of the joint, he was trying to cleanse himself of all that was past. Of course, it was to improve the quality of his own life, but his main motive was the love of a woman. Thank God for Becca. They'd only dated a few weeks before getting married and moving here to White Falls. It was to be a happily ever after for this monster-gone-marital, but the nightmares began day one...

"Doc, I don't know what the hell gasping for air in complete darkness has to do with me being insecure. I mean, insecure about what?" Frustrated and sleepless, Tom sank further down into the gray leather couch.

Dr. Sarah looked up from her notes, "Well, perhaps the helpless feeling represents your feelings of inadequacy as a husband to a woman with a more...wholesome upbringing." She removed her glasses to speak more directly. "Mr. Malcolm, you can't tell me that you don't have a bit of an inferiority complex."

Tom threw his hands up and shook his head, "Listen, I know what I was and I know what I am, alright? Shit, lady! You act like I come home and resent my wife for growing up decent!"

Dr. Sarah raised her hand to cease his rant. "Mr. Malcolm, I'm merely suggesting that you probably don't experience day-to-day as a normal person would. Each day, I'm sure, is a challenge to reconnect with the outside and there have to be insecurities that go along with that, correct?"

Tom looked at the floor before conceding, "Yeah...yeah I suppose you're right." Smiling, Dr. Sarah stood up and started towards her large oak desk at the back of the room. She pulled an RX pad from the drawer.

"Mr. Malcolm," she began as she scribbled, "I'm going to up your dose of Melatinol." With that, she tore the square note from the pad and made her way back to the couch. "This increase should help with the anxiety, which will hopefully bring an end to your sleepless nights."

Biting his lip, Tom nodded. She gave a reassuring smile as he took the prescription from her hand. "Now," she said, "I want to see a well-rested man in two weeks. No more nightmares, hm?"

"I certainly hope so, Doc." Tom rose from the couch and followed her to the door. "This is wreakin' some mad havoc on my sex life."

The doctor chuckled, "Make that a well-rested and well-satisfied man." Tom made his way through the hallway and to the elevator, where a woman and her young daughter stepped aside to make room. When the elevator chimed, he took notice of the small redheaded girl staring intently at him. He smiled and gave a small wave, but her look was unwavering. Tom raised an eyebrow to her. "Jesus, this town..." he thought to himself.

When the elevator opened Tom darted for the revolving door, drawing out his cigarettes and lighting one in a fit of restlessness once he was outside. He closed his eyes to take a long drag. Exhaling deep, he reopened them on a bus stop bench where an elderly woman sat, scowling at him. He shot her back a look. Slowly, she turned back around, and he rolled his eyes as he took another hit. "What the fuck?" he whispered.

Flicking his cigarette to the concrete, Tom swung open the door of his red Taurus and plopped into the driver's seat. He slammed the door and bent forward to rest his exhausted head on the steering wheel. After a few moments he leaned back, shook out his hair, then placed the key in the ignition. Upon the start, industrial rock poured through the speakers.

He drove his way through the winding roads and

looked out at Puritan river, the water that surrounded White Falls. Over the city loomed a large chemical plant with smoke barreling from the stacks. The large sign in front read: "Cleaner Energy for our children and future: Blanc Industries." Tom chuckled as he lit another cigarette and rolled down the window, "Well, your future reeks of shit, I'll tell ya that."

Cigarette steadfast in his mouth, he turned into Trent's Market, parked, and sent a text to Becca:

> Done at witch doctor. Need N E thing from the store?

Her response was prompt:

> You're out of ham for your lunch. Unless you want one of my Trim Cuisines. ;)

He smiled as he typed:

> Mmm frozen broccoli.

He received a smiley in response.

A cool rush of citrusy air hit his senses when the grocery doors parted. A man looked up from gathering grapefruits into a plastic baggie. He stopped dead as their eyes met. Tom broke from his stare to yank a cart free from the rest. Muttering some colorful vocabulary, he rolled his way to the pharmacy.

A middle-aged man in black was walking towards him. As he came closer, Tom took notice of his white collar. To Tom's surprise, the man smiled at him and extended his hand. "You must be Tom," he said, shaking his hand. "Welcome to White Falls, Mr. Malcolm!"

"Wow, a warm reception. That's refreshing!"

"Aw, I assure you this town is filled with many a warm heart." He leaned in to whisper, "The older folks are just quick to judge, but they'll come around."

"Man, I hope so, Father...?"

"Oh, I'm sorry— I'm Father McLaughlin of the church over on Waxen road."

Tom nodded, "Well hey, it's sure nice to meet someone like you. I mean, I get the cold shoulder around here. Guess news travels fast when you're a convict." Father McLaughlin waved his hand dismissingly, "Bah! It'd travel fast even if your past was all sunshine and roses. This place is just small, that's all. Not enough to jabber on about."

Tom drew a sigh, "I suppose…"

"Listen," the priest interrupted. "These people need to remember that sometimes people fall short of glory."

"Yes. And thank you for saying so."

The priest gave a firm slap to his arm, "Think nothing of it, my friend. Maybe I'll see you Sunday."

"Just maybe, Father."

Father McLaughlin turned and started towards the dairy section. But just as Tom went to resume his shopping, the priest stopped suddenly and turned back around. "Oh, and one more thing, Tom."

Tom looked over, giving the priest his full attention.

"Don't, uh..." he started. "Well, just be cautious about drinking the tap water."

Tom cocked his head inquisitively.

"You see, there are a lot of chemicals that get dumped into the Puritan and..." He stopped short, realizing the awkwardness that consumed the moment. Raising his head, he smiled with confidence and decided to kill the thought with, "Just trust me on this one. OK, Tom?"

The two men went down separate aisles, and Tom skipped picking up bread, since the priest was busying himself reading all of the hamburger bun labels. He paid for his groceries and got into his car. The sun was setting over the water when Tom pulled up to his house to see Becca's silhouette through the shades of their colonial home. It was nice to know she was there, after the day's oddities. He smiled for a moment, watching her form waltz back and forth in front of the window. She often paced when she hadn't seen him all day, though she'd never let on.

He made his way up the cobblestone steps, grocery bag in hand. He opened the door to find Becca still in her hospital scrubs. Her blonde bob swung as she turned around. He practically ran towards her and grabbed her up in his arms.

She laughed, "Well, hello!"

He set her down and looked into her eyes, "You have no idea how happy I am to be home." He planted a firm kiss on her lips before walking past to the fridge. "Tell me something, Becca," he said, setting the bag down and grabbing a soda. "How did you grow up in this town and make it out normal?"

"Normal? I wouldn't go that far. Why—what the hell happened, anyway?"

Tom took a long swig. "Damn, I wish this was a beer," he said aloud to himself. "How did I let you convince me to come to a dry county?"

Becca wrapped her arms around his waist and smiled up at him, "Because you love me and because you know I always wanted to come back home."

Tom rolled his eyes as he pet her head, "That's right."

"And besides," she began again. "You came here for a fresh start. Boozin' is a part of what put you in that awful place, remember?"

Tom took a sip as he looked on in brief reflection. He gave her a smirk, "You're lucky you're cute."

They exchanged a smile before another kiss, then started for the living room hand in hand. Settling with him on the couch, Becca asked, "What'd the doctor have to say, baby?"

"Well..." he set the soda on the coffee table, "There's no hope. Surgery isn't going to fix this ugly." His wife narrowed her eyes and pursed her lips."Okay. She gave me a higher dosage of that anti-anxiety stuff. Shit, I'd take rhino tranquilizer if I knew it'd help me sleep."

Becca smiled and leaned in towards him. "Alright, I'm going to take my shower and go to bed, babe." They shared a kiss.

"Yup, I'll be in there soon." He scooped the remote from the coffee table. Crossing his legs, he sank further into the couch and flipped the television on. He went to take a swig from his soda but stopped midway when he noticed the man on screen.

It was Father McLaughlin. He was standing in front of Puritan River speaking to a news crew about the community. In the background, Blanc Industries shined like a beacon against the sunset. Although the volume was set low, Tom could faintly make out words like "progress" and "family."

"Honey? Honey, I met this guy today in the store!" He waited a few seconds before calling her name again. No answer, just the shower. Turning to face the program once more, his body nearly jerked from the couch.

Father McLaughlin's face was staring directly into the camera, straight at him.

Tom rubbed his eyes and refocused, thinking maybe the screen had frozen. After his eyes settled, he took note of the waves still moving in the background as strands of the priest's hair blew about in the wind. His dark eyes stared at Tom from the illuminated plasma screen. Tom cocked his head and his brows sank deep, then he blinked and shook his head in disbelief, "What the hell is this?" He grabbed the remote and pressed the "change channel" button. Indeed it changed...only to reveal the same image.

He clicked the button a few more times; each time, Father McLaughlin stared. Tom swallowed hard and his right leg began to shake. He nervously called for his wife again, "Becca? ...Becca?!"

Still nothing.

He turned to face the screen again. The priest's mouth had dropped opened and his jaw became lax as he shut his eyes and tipped his head back. His mouth continued to widen as greasy black leathery figures danced around his tongue. He could hear the sound of Father McLaughlin's mucus thickening against the outer membrane of the beings like hordes of maggots writhing in the rot. "What the fu—AAAAH!"

Tom sprang up from their bed. His face glistened and beads of sweat began to roll down his face. Realizing it was just another nightmare, he helplessly dropped his head in his hands. Becca rolled over from her slumber to console him, "Did you forget to take your pills, baby?"

Tom's hands shook over his face as he struggled to regain composure. He shuffled his thoughts for a few moments. Nothing made sense. He breathed a deep sigh and turned his face from his trembling hands to face her. He wore the look of a terrified child. "I don't know."

* * * *

Later that afternoon, Tom begrudgingly straightened his red tie over his white collared shirt. With a day of delivering spiels about high-speed internet ahead of him, he longed to climb back into bed. The thought crossed his mind as he squeezed a spot of toothpaste onto his brush. He drew a heavy sigh when his second thought promptly cancelled out his first. Bed was a hell too. No matter where he turned, he was damned to torture with no relief in sight.

Don't think that the third thought wasn't one that involved a bullet.

"Oh, hello Mr. Peterson! I just wanted to know on a scale of one to ten, how satisfied you are with your current internet speed?"

click

Tom whipped off his headphones in a fury and plopped them onto the keyboard. He rubbed his eyes. Spinning in his chair, he turned to face the cubicle across the hall. "Kelly, I'm goin' to lunch."

On a day like today, he'd be dining on a lukewarm soda and a coupla smokes. He ran his fingers through his slicked hair, creating shaggy locks. Opening the car door, he plopped into the driver's seat and slammed it with an angsty sneer. Closing his eyes, he reached blindly for the cup holder and grabbed his warm soda. After a swig of the flat caramel-colored liquid, he finger punched the power button on the stereo, scanning the channels for a decent rock station. What he found instead was all ministries.

"And He will bring a balance to this universe like none have ever—"

"The wicked will bow before Him and justice will prevail over—"

"Bestia, ave dominus!"

Tom shook his head in disgust and utter confusion before he switched off the stereo and slammed himself back into the seat. "What is this shit?! Now I gotta listen to this Bible bullshit?! Is this the fuckin' Twilight Zone?! GOD!"

He tilted his head back, closed his eyes, and firmly pinched his nose. That bullet was sounding mighty tasty right about now. After his breathing had slowed down, Tom picked up on a low electric hum from the speakers. He glanced to the stereo to confirm that he'd shut it off.

He had.

The hum continued, and he looked around to see what might be making the noise. He sank low in his seat to get a better view of the speakers and car floor. Finding nothing, he sat up again — eye level with Father McLaughlin through the driver window. Tom jumped and shook the car, "Jesus!"

The priest's intent stare did not waiver. His eyes remained cold and steadfast on Tom's. Tom took a few seconds and collected himself before yelling, "Well? WHAT DO YOU WANT?!"

The priest grinned as his eyes widened. He responded, "Your judgment." Tom frowned, and when he tried to open the car door found that it wouldn't budge. He rocked against it in efforts to free himself. He pounded on the door as the priest grinned in mockery of the situation.

Tom was already feeling helpless when a sharp, teeth-clenching pain shot through his spine. The pain was like his flesh tearing; a pain that would make a grown man cry out for death. His ears rang profusely as the searing heat tore through his limbs, and he found himself soaked in sweat. He clenched onto his chest while he thrashed and screamed.

The priest continued to smile, watching Tom drip sweat and writhe in agony. Tom tried to reach for the center console to grab his keys, but the knifelike pain in his arms did not allow him to coordinate thusly; his arms could not release their hold on the steering wheel.

Just as the blood vessels began to break over his sweat-ridden eyeballs, his stomach began to bloat and protrude. The pain sent him into a seizure. His eyes rolled back and his mouth began to foam just as his skin on his stomach reached maximum stretch before ripping...

Tom awoke in a pool of sweat in his marital bed. His head jerked to the left, looking for the clock. Two am. The red numbers were partially covered by a semi-translucent post-it that read: "Emergency surgery. Got called into work." Tom's face remained frozen, his eyes locked on the numbers. Had he even gone to work? His body began to tremble out of helpless fear. With quivering lips, he tightly closed his eyes. He began to wail uncontrollably. He wanted so badly to make a swift exit from this reality.

He wanted to die.

Tom shivered, awake in his damp sheets, and was a mess of tears for at least twenty minutes. He coughed and wailed like a lost child until he could barely breathe. Sputtering, he ran his hands through his sweaty chopped locks in an attempt to catch his breath. Once at last he did, he sat up slowly and scooted his back towards the headboard. He could not hold up his own sleepless, limp body.

He was dead weight.

While his raggedy form lay propped against that headboard, he caught his reflection in the mirror to right of their bed. He almost didn't recognize it. What he saw was a man who looked a decade his senior, his hair flecked with white and silver. The bags under his eyes hung just beneath the red slits in his face that housed his eyeballs. His mind was aging him, torturing him, and slowly killing him.

Turning away from the hideous stranger, he stared forward into the dark nothingness. It was then he gave himself an ultimatum: find a way to fight this or give in to a bullet. The prescription pills remained untouched, collecting dust on the bathroom sink. How can he take them when he can't keep track of time? Sections of his day were completely erased from memory. Staring into the darkness, he thought of Father McLaughlin. It was time to pay him a visit.

Dawn seeped its way through the bay windows, and Tom's eyes began to ache. The light was quite literally a sight for sore eyes. He watched the beams climbed over his balled-up khakis on the wood floor. With slothlike hesitance, he moved the sheets and began to climb out of bed. He reached down with a shaky, unsteady hand to his wrinkled pants. He pulled them in as he swung his legs around to place his bare feet on the cold floor, the coolness sending chills through him. His raw nerves made his whole being hypersensitive.

It took nearly ten minutes, but one leg at a time he managed to step into his pants and stand. He didn't bother changing his sweaty undershirt. He needed a cigarette, bad. He slipped on some loafers, grabbed the keys, lit a smoke, and was in his car.

The five-mile drive seemed like an eternity. He had no idea what he was going to say to the priest, but he had to find out why these dreams were occurring. Tom pulled into the parking lot of the quaint stone church that sat on the river. He could faintly make out the smoke stacks from Blanc Industries in the distance beyond it. No steeples or bells, just a grey stone cottage and a charming marquee. There he was at seven am on a Wednesday in an empty church lot. He hadn't set foot on church grounds since he was a boy, when his grandfather died. He and Becca had gotten married in a wedding chapel, which would never constitute as a place of worship.

The car idled as he sat, in dead silence, waiting. He

let the AC blast him in the face so as not to nod off. An hour later, a black windowless van rolled into the lot. It looked like an armory company had just arrived, but he knew it was Father McLaughlin.

Tom shuddered seeing the priest exit his vehicle. There he was. The man who gave the most welcome only to give the worst haunting. How could this be? The priest looked towards Tom's car with a big smile and waved enthusiastically, then signaled for him to follow him into the church. Tom watched as Father McLaughlin unlocked the door and stepped inside. With a face of stone, Tom turned off the ignition and trudged his way up the cobblestone path. One way or another, he was determined to find out just what the hell was going on. This day was going to bring about some sense, goddammit.

Father McLaughlin greeted him in the empty hallway with arms wide, pulling him in for a hearty hug, "Great to see you, my boy!" He ignored Tom's arms hanging limply at his side. "You're about an hour early for service, but that's quite alright!" After a few pats on the back, he pushed Tom back to get a look at his face, and drew a sharp breath when he saw Tom's lifeless glare. "My God, boy. Are you alright?"

Tom sighed as he rubbed the back of his neck, "I haven't been sleeping well, Father." Father McLaughlin took notice of the awkward tension and gave a look of concern, "Well, I'm sorry to say but it's visually apparent. Step into my office, son. Take a load off."

Tom followed him down the dark hallway and into an open area just before the chapel. Even in his sleepy stupor, he was able to take note of some oddities. The walls were a flat gray, and completely blank. No crosses, no stained glass, no religious accents of any kind. He panned around curiously as they walked, "Did you just move into the building, Father?"

The priest reached into his black slacks for his keys as they approached a large wooden door. "Well, about three years ago, maybe." He crashed the keys against the knob. "The secretary was supposed to get on to decorating, but funding is a bit tight."

"Well, I'm sure God doesn't need bells and whistles."

The priest didn't respond but rather just smiled as the office door swung open. He stepped aside to let Tom pass, "After you."

Book cases lined the walls, and reached from floor to ceiling. They were stuffed to the brim. After Father McLaughlin switched on the light behind him, Tom could see a large oak desk towards the far wall. Even more interesting was a small glass fish tank sitting on a table near the window behind the desk. No fish, but rather some slimy black shadows. The silhouettes dashed from one end of the tank to the other.

"Have a seat at the desk, Tom."

Tom did his best to ease into the worn red oak chair. It looked like it had been inherited from a 1940s banker. The priest took his place in the large, leather office chair directly across from Tom, leaning forward and resting his arms on the desk, "What ails you, my boy, and how can I be of assistance?"

Tom sighed heavily and his eyes searched around for a thought. Some dialogue had played out in his head in the car. When the moment came, however, it failed to project into reality. There were no words. How do you tell a man you barely know that he's everything your nightmares are made of? Tom's eyes continued to wander. Jesus, what to say...

"Listen," Father McLaughlin took this awkward silence as an opportunity to reach a common understanding, "I know it's been a struggle for you since you've been here. The townsfolk whisper and give cold shoulders." Tom closed his eyes tightly as the priest went on. "And I know it may be hard being the striped among the righteous—"

"Wait," Tom interrupted. "These people ain't no better than me. I mean, we're all human and we're all equal."

"Equal?" the priest scoffed. "Enlighten me, Tom. What does that word mean to you?"

Tom cocked his head and squinted in confusion. He was taken aback by the change in the priest's tone. "Now, just how am I supposed to answer that, Father?"

"Equal would mean of the same degree and standard." He shook his head scornfully, "No, my boy. If we were all of the same, 'equal' righteous nature, we'd already be living in the heavenly bliss that my congregation strives for every day."

Tom couldn't help but wear a put-off appearance. He couldn't bring about a rebuttal because he wasn't quite sure of the argument proposed. Just what was this man driving at? Father McLaughlin rose swiftly and took a few steps towards the small aquarium behind him. "Do you know anything about leeches, Tom?"

"I, uh...know they're blood suckers."

"Ah, close!" the priest exclaimed, turning from the tank to face him. "They're used in old world medicine to suck the IMPURE blood." He slowly submerged his hand wrist-deep into the murky water. Tom sat frozen in his seat. Perhaps this was a dream, as well.

After a brief silence, Father McLaughlin raised his hand out of the water to reveal it adorned with thin, shiny worms. "The old world was a place where the righteous were more prevalent, not outnumbered like they are now." He rotated his wrist as he examined it. "It is up to us, Tom, to restore the universal balance of good and evil. Up to us to take back our place in the world— in the heavens." Thin streams of blood slowly rained from the Father's leech-ridden hand onto the dusty wood floor.

Tom stood from his seat. "Listen, Father. Whatever it is that you're trying to say, just save it. I've seen and heard enough." He turned and started for the door, muttering, "Crazy fuck."

He reached for the brass knob, but the heavy wooden door creaked loudly as it swung open before him. There was his wife, standing in the hallway in her hospital scrubs. She wore a look of concern and pity. Tom shook his head in disbelief, "Becca? Wha—what are you doing here?"

Stopping just a few inches from him, Becca raised her head to meet his eyes. "Restoring the balance." She grasped the back of his head and pressed a white cloth to his mouth and nose, gripping tighter as they both crashed to their knees. Tom's limbs thrashed about, and he let out a strangled sob. His vision became a blurred mess of lights and flashes of Becca's face, and his body fell limp in her arms.

* * * *

Tom could faintly make out large pine trees passing in and out of sight as he came to. He felt the touch of cold wet mud on his back, and then the small sudden jabs of his body rolling over rocks and pebbles. All at once, full consciousness hit him. He was being dragged.

His arms were extended above him, his wrists tightly bound and rubbed raw by thick rope. There were people near him; familiar faces. The townspeople were marching alongside his moving body. Among the faces were Dr. Sarah, the scowling old woman, and the small redheaded girl from the elevator. A large grunt of a man was hauling him through the woods, the jowls that made up his neck sweating profusely. His mangled teeth could be seen through his bouts of mouth breathing. A personified swine.

And then there was Becca.

She looked at him cold. She wore a stranger's eyes as if she did not know him at all. From the previous events, it was clear he didn't know her at all either.

Suddenly, he heard Father McLaughlin's voice echo in the distance, "And He will bring a balance to this universe like none have ever seen!"

The townspeople responded in monotone unison, "Grando autem in bestia."

"The wicked will bow before Him and justice will prevail over the human race!"

Again they responded, "Grando autem in bestia."

A mixture of fear and helplessness took over as Tom looked at Becca once more. "Becca! Becca, please!"

She gave him an empty look. A look that reassured him he was truly alone in this fight. He strained against the ropes on his ankles to no avail. There was nothing he could do now.

As the trees cleared to reveal the open gray sky, he heard the sounds of choppy river water. The pig-man dropped his arms and the congregation came to a halt. Tom tried to lower his wrists, but the grunt pounced on them with his steel toe boots instead, completely shattering the left.

Tom screamed in wild agony. Through his tears, he could make out Father McLaughlin standing over him and addressing his attacker, "I said restrain him, not hurt him! We cannot treat wicked with wickedness. We are here to purify, not to fight fire with fire." He placed a hand on the man's shoulder, "Never lose sight of why we do this, son. Understood?" The pig-man nodded in shamefaced agreement.

The priest looked into Tom's tormented eyes and

smiled. "Today, Tom, you will be doing society a great service. Your sacrifice will bring us further to achieving heaven on earth by picking up the justice system's slack—"

Tom wasn't listening. He could do nothing but cry as he begged for his life, "Please! DON'T DO THIS! PLEASE!"

His sobs fell on deaf ears. Father McLaughlin walked away from him, reaching out and exchanging words with some of the townspeople, and the pig-man grabbed him up roughly by the forearms and dragged him to a metal railing overhanging the water.

His head was propped against the cold metal as he watched the priest take a coil of rope from Dr. Sarah and make his way back to Tom's ragged body. Father McLaughlin used the rope to wrap Tom's wrists further, ignoring the shrieks of pain when he banged against his shattered left wrist. This time, the roped reached down his forearms. After tightly securing his handiwork with a sailor's knot, Father McLaughlin took the rest of the slacked rope and tied it to the railing with the same knot. It was a good ten minutes before he stood back to observe his work. He nodded. Without hesitation and without ceremony, the ogre tossed Tom's body over the edge.

Tom screamed as the rope tore skin from his forearm and pulled his right shoulder from its socket. He dangled there over the water, his dark blood soaking through the binding rope. He screamed again, crying for help through the nauseating pain. Looking out over the choppy waters, he saw the chemical plant. Through his blurred vision, he made out the sign once again: "Cleaner Energy for our children and future. Blanc Industries."

Clean. White. Pure. The future.

His panicked mind kept him from noticing the water

below becoming a mess of violent waves. That is, until he felt vibrations through the cement wall at his back; it was like a submarine was broaching. Then he caught glimpses of a large volcanic-black figure between the waves.

Picking up speed, it began to rise from the water—a giant, black leathery being as wide as a jet liner. Faster and faster, it rose before Tom, reaching a height of fifty feet into the air when it straightened out. Unwinding from its bent form, it ceased movement. For a moment, Tom looked at the serpent-like monster seething in front of him, and then his bottom lip began to tremor uncontrollably. Then his whole body shook. Tears ran from eyes that glazed from sheer horror. He shook his head in denial of what he was seeing. Tom was now staring into the face of this beast, this eyeless, rubbery being.

A large horizontal slit began to open on the beast's face. It widened slowly to reveal a row of silver, razorlike teeth. Tom tried to scream in response to this unholy terror, but when he opened his mouth to let it escape, he just vomited violently. He thrashed his body wildly in the wind as the beast's slit widened further, exposing a second row of teeth...

HIS MAJESTY PART I

"Will you do me this great honor?"

Linda traced the frame of their engagement snapshot on the pier. No wonder he had suggested she curl her hair that day, passing it off as if he had a preference. He knew how she felt about her photo being taken. Next to the arrival of their twin girls, it had been the best day of her life. From age five, she had painted pictures of lake houses, hoping one day she'd reside in one. He saw to it that her dreams were fulfilled. Rick was selfless like that. The best husband anyone could ask for.

She placed the frame back on the mantel before turning to face him. There he sat on the couch staring blankly at the television. His once stocky, built frame and shaggy blonde locks had faded into a frail bald man almost overnight. He sat slumped on their brown leather sofa fixated on Game Hunters. You couldn't reach him if you tried. He was in the same place she left him last night. Though he was alive when she said goodnight. Saying good morning to a dead man damn near killed her.

"Daddy!" Seven-year-olds Lucy and Lisa ran in their oversized flannel gowns to give their father his good morning bear hug. The girls were his spitting image despite having their mother's auburn hair.

He didn't respond nor did he budge; he maintained his steady blank stare on the screen. Lisa climbed onto her dad's lap as his slim frame slumped. Gently petting his bald head, she asked, "Daddy, are you sad?"

He did not answer.

Linda shot a look of concern at the figure on the couch. "Girls, Daddy's havin' a day, okay? He'll be alright." She forced a smile. "Why don't you both wash your hands and get ready for breakfast, hm?"

The girls gave their father a squeeze before scurrying to the bathroom, and their mother sighed heavily as she started for the kitchen. Reaching into the cabinet above the coffeepot, she took out two mugs. She shook the packet of Sweet'N Low before adding it to her cup. Pouring the coffee, she flashed to their first date at the Pearl Perk. She recalled that the afternoon had turned into an amazing evening, twelve years ago. She looked up for a moment and chuckled remembering his reaction to her adding artificial sweetener: "Jesus, don't cha know that shit'll kill ya?"

At that moment, the barista placed a large cinnamon roll — with extra frosting — on the table before him. There was a brief, silent pause before laughter erupted between them. Of course, she'd never forget the words that followed, "Linda, if you never go on another date with my asshole-self, I want you to know that seeing your gorgeous smile today was more than worth it."

Standing there at the kitchen counter, she placed her hand over her mouth to regain composure. She'd give up all she owned just to hear him say that one last time.

Before the tears could fall, the girls entered the

kitchen and took their places at the table. Linda quickly choked down her moment and reached atop the fridge for the Pony Puffs. Cereal in hand, she swung open the fridge door, scooped up the milk carton, and set both on the table before the girls. "There ya go," she said, turning back to the coffee.

Lucy piped up. "Um, Momma?"

"WHAT?"

The girls were clearly taken aback; she didn't usually snap at them like that. Linda softened her demeanor, saying "I'm sorry, honey. I shouldn't have snapped like that." She looked at the half-set breakfast table. "Oh—oops! Bowls and spoons might help!" Linda grabbed what they needed and smiled, "There you go, sweeties."

The twins smiled back, dismissing their mother's unusual behavior.

Linda grabbed the coffee cups and started for the living room, placing his cup on the wooden table before taking her place beside him. She gently placed her hand on his thigh. "Y'know, your mother called this morning, worried… I told her you were still asleep. She wants you to call her back later."

He did not acknowledge her.

She looked above the television to gaze at their engagement photo again. A beachgoer had taken it for them. It was so damned windy in Scarborough that day. She remembered pushing her hair out of her face in time to catch him taking to one knee. He clutched onto his navy polo just over his heart. "Linda, there are no words to explain how much you mean to me. You're simply…you're the reason I breathe. I don't ever want to live another moment without you."

Her eyes welled with tears as he reached into his pocket, pulled out a blue velvet box, opened it, and presented the emerald solitaire. She paid no mind to the ring, but stared into his eyes as he asked, "Will you do me this great honor? Will you be my wife?"

Linda broke from reminiscing to glance over at the feeble shell that sat beside her. She took a quiet sip of coffee before starting in again, "The shop is going to slow down even more now that you're... like this. It's really gonna be hard to make ends meet at a taxidermy shop when the only thing I'm good at is the raccoons."

More silence.

Exasperated, she set her cup on the coffee table. "You simply can't do this. Not the girls, not to me. To us. This isn't fair." Her breathing began to quicken and her lips quivered. "You told me you'd be there for us no matter what."

He was stone.

The phone broke the moment. Linda stood quickly and marched to the kitchen. She damn near jerked the thing from the wall before speaking into the receiver, "Hello?!...Yes, this is Mrs. Adkins...He did? Oh, I'm sorry. He must have forgotten. Can I call back to reschedule?...Yes, the doctor said he was switching to the other Chemo...right...right." Linda bit her lip and closed her eyes tight. "Mm-hm. Yes, I understand...I'll call back as soon as possible...Yep. Uh-huh. Bye, now."

She hung up and stalked back into the living room. "Well Rick, you missed your appointment this morning."

He stared at the TV.

She lost it. Frustrated by his lack of response, she grabbed him up by the collar. His head slumped to one side as she yelled, "Rick, you don't understand! You can't just leave me here! Do you hear me?!" Still gripping his undershirt, she began to cry, "Listen! Listen to me, dammit! YOU—CAN'T—JUST—LEAVE—US! I can't believe you'd die like this!"

"Mom?"

She raised her tear-stained face to her frightened

daughters cowering in the kitchen doorway. Quickly sobering from the moment, she released his collar slowly as he sank back onto the couch. "It's okay, girls. Daddy and I were just talking."

The twins stared back at their mother with bowed heads.

Linda scooped up her coffee mug and forced another smile. "Hey, do you know what weekend it is?"

The girls' faces lit up. "GRANDMA SUE'S HOUSE!"

"That's right! Put your dishes in the sink and let's get ready!"

The girls quickly ran off. Dishes clattered in the sink and there were the sounds of teeth-brushing and dresser drawers slamming while Linda tried to collect herself. Trembling, she took a step towards her husband and started to reach for his wrist. She stopped, and just stared at him instead. With that last pitiful look, she made her way down the hall to help her daughters.

With fresh clothes and braided pigtails, Lucy and Lisa dragged their bags to the front door and slipped on their coats. Lisa looked at her mother, saying, "We gotta say bye to Daddy, Momma."

"Your Daddy's...sleeping, honey."

"I'll just whisper it, then."

The girls crept quietly to the couch. They each whispered, "Goodbye, Daddy....love you." Pressing her fist to her mouth, Linda took a breath before the girls ran past her on their way to the minivan, yelling behind them, "C'mon, Mom!"

Uncomfortable silence ensued as they made their way down the winding roads. Lucy finally broke the quiet, "Mom, is Daddy gonna be okay?"

Linda spoke to their inquisitive faces through the rear view, "Yes. Daddy will be okay." Reassured, the girls quietly took in the scenery of the changing fall leaves until they pulled onto their grandmother's gravel drive.

A short, gray-haired woman in a hoodie and blue jeans waved from the wooden porch steps. Linda had barely put it in park when the girls swung open the van doors and ran towards their grandmother. "GRANDMA SUE!"

"Hey, hey princesses!" Grandma Sue knelt down to catch their hugs. "Oh, you give Grandma the best bear hugs!" She gently pushed their shoulders back to meet their faces, and whispered discretely, "How's your mom and dad?"

"Momma's getting our stuff out of the van," Lisa responded, "and Daddy's been sleeping ALL DAY!"

As their mother walked up with their bags she smiled at Grandma Sue. "Hello, mother!"

"Hey sweetie, so good to see you!" Sue said. "How's Rick feeling?"

Linda set the bags on the porch and pushed her hair from her face. "He's...very tired."

"The side effects of the chemo, I'm sure." Sue studied Linda for a moment. "Don't you worry, dear."

"I don't," Linda smiled. "Just keepin' the faith and prayin,' y'know?"

"That's all we can do. We'll get through this."

Linda nodded in agreement and gave her mother-in-law a hug before kissing her girls goodbye, "You two be good for Grandma Sue, okay?" The girls nodded emphatically before darting into the house. "Call if you need me, Mom."

"I'm sure we'll be just fine," Sue said, giving Linda another searching look. "It's you I worry about, dear."

Finally alone, Linda broke down into sobs about a mile down the road. She pounded the steering wheel; she screamed and cried so hard she could barely see. Surely this wasn't happening. This was not her life. This was not how it was supposed to be.

Then, suddenly, she heard them. Whispers.

She quickly glanced around to find no one. Feeling clumsily over the dash, she checked to make sure the radio wasn't on.

The whispers continued the whole way home, and she listened intently.

He left you last night, Linda. He left you here.

They spoke directly to her. It was a female's voice...it was her own voice. She shook her head in disbelief. Surely, she was imagining this.

He's gone. You let him leave.

The girls will be devastated... you know that, right?

"Shut UP!"

What's the matter, Linda?

Didn't plan on being widowed at thirty-two?

Feeling sorry for yourself?

"STOP IT! STOP!"

Linda pulled the car to a stop alongside the woods. She rested her head against the steering wheel and began to wail. The whispers finally ceased.

It was quiet.

In that brief moment of relief, she looked up to notice a deer just a few feet in front of the van. It stopped still and gazed directly at her. She shifted, thinking it would stir. It didn't. It kept a steady stare just as Rick did that morning. It was in that moment that things suddenly became clear.

She knew how she could keep him.

She knew how to preserve his place in the family, how to maintain his presence in the home.

She didn't want to be alone, and she wouldn't have to be, if she could preserve his...majesty.

With that realization, Linda pulled back onto the road in a hurry. She floored it the rest of the way home, laughing victoriously. "I'm comin' home, babe! We're gonna fix this! HaHA!" She roared onto the gravel driveway and threw it in park. Turning off the ignition, she jumped out of the van and ran through the side screen door. "Honey! I'm hooome!"

Her lifeless husband was in the living room looking a bit bloated and bruised as if he'd been in a scrap.

"Don't worry, baby, we can fix that. No problem!"

Linda jetted out the door, running towards the shed where they skinned their large game and flinging open its wooden double doors. The thick steel chains that hung from the ceiling chimed with the breeze. She looked at the two large silver bloodstained hooks that dragged across the floor and smiled with delight.

"Yes. Yes! This is gonna work!"

Bracing herself against the doors, she glanced around for any potential onlookers. Not having neighbors was just another bonus for them. They'd always enjoyed the privacy the lakefront property offered.

Back in the house, Linda dragged the coffee table away from Rick. She bent down and swung his hundred-pound body over her shoulder trudging a few steps before collapsing in the hallway. He was light, but he was still deadweight.

His corpse lay sprawled on her body for a few moments as she caught her breath. She managed to commando-crawl from underneath him and decided to drag him by the arms instead. Grasping his wrists, she flipped him onto his back and proceeded to drag his body across the wood floor and through the hall. When they reached the door, she propped it open with one foot, trying not to bang him up too badly.

It was smooth sailing once they reached the grass. She lifted his arms slightly when they reached the shed so as not to knock his head against the concrete floor.

Once his body was in, she reached for the doors, closed them, and slammed down the long wooden lock.

Looking him over, Linda's logic was to treat him as a mammoth raccoon. She walked to the far wall and picked up a scalpel from the wooden table. Starting at his white undershirt, she made an incision at the collar and ripped the rest from his chest. His flannel pajama bottoms and boxers proved to be an easy slip-off. His bony, shriveled, pale, naked body lay before her with bloated gut.

Without hesitation, she raised one hook and stabbed it through his left Achilles tendon. Blood spurted onto the floor from the speedy impact. She proceeded to strike the right with the other hook. After wiping her bloody hands on her husband's shirt, she tossed the blood soaked rag in the corner and then started pulling the chains with all her body strength. The bag of flesh that was once Rick began to rise slowly from the floor until it was suspended in the air. He swung as the burgundy blood from his ankles ran freely down his legs and over his groin. Locking the chains in place, she began to prep for his skinning.

The scalpel gave a metallic ring when she grabbed it from the table. She stopped suddenly to survey his suspended body, and she remembered out loud,

"The hands have to be removed to in order to get a clean sweep of the skin from the tissue."

Linda put the scalpel back down and scooped up a small axe instead. Kneeling down, she grabbed Rick's right hand.

"This won't hurt, baby. I promise."

His blood rained onto her face as she hacked at his wrist. It felt as if she were chopping into a raw beef roast. The blade stuck into the muscle tissue between blows, and she had to wiggle the axe to free it from his half-hacked wrist. As his blood drained onto the floor, she proceeded with the same technique to the left hand. Standing in a pool of her husband's blood, she grabbed up his hands and tossed them across the shed. She took a step back to witness the draining of her now handless late husband and caught her breath.

It was going to be a long weekend.

The blood began to clot and thicken around the part of his head that grazed the cement. His scalp was stained as auburn as his wife's locks. Still standing a few feet away, she pointed and made gestures with the scalpel she'd grabbed again. She spoke aloud to refresh her memory.

"Feet, medial legs, groin."

She bent down and set the knife on the floor next to her before removing her shoes and socks. Retrieving the knife, she walked back to him and stepped her bare feet into his mucousy, red sea. Wading in it, she reached up for his left foot and grasped it tightly as she made a deep incision along the lateral side. After tracing his toes, she carefully ran the blade through the inner side and over the top of his ankle. Blood dripped over his feet like teardrops where she'd carved. Running over the superficial skin of his ankle, she began to speak aloud.

"Remember when your father got sick at our wedding and blamed it on the shrimp cocktail?"

Her hand braced his calf as she pressed deeper, running along his tibia.

"I was so emotional that day, Rick. It seemed like nothing went right."

Her husband's body swung as she readjusted to start along his knee.

"You said that the only thing you needed to go right already happened. You had found me."

She smiled.

Gracefully, she slid the blade over his inner thigh before meeting his perineum. His right leg bore thin beaded blood lines that stemmed out like branches over his flesh. Below her feet, the skin on his handless arms began to pucker and shrivel like leather. Close up, it looked like swine flesh being dried out for jerky.

She grasped his scrotum to hold his body in place as she slid the blade up through the left inner thigh. After repeating the same process, she went back and forth between legs, making a few long incisions from the outer ankle up and down through the hip along the buttocks.

She knew the part that would require the most physical exertion was up next. She dropped her arms and the scalpel fell to the ground, chiming happily while she caught her breath. Linda looked like she'd been baptized in blood. When she wiped the sweat from her brow she only added Rick's blood to her own perspiration. Her hands were soaked to the wrist.

Slowly she reached up to his right toes and placed her fingertips between them. Bracing his foot with her other hand, she dug her nails into the incision she'd made and began to tear downward. Closing her eyes, she mustered the strength to tear the stubborn skin from his flesh.

With each tug, she exposed more raw muscle tissue. Between each tear, though, she struggled. Her hands were slipping; several times she had to stop to adjust her grip. Once at his knee, she grasped his skin with both hands as she raised herself from the floor. It took all her body weight to get it over his bony patella. Once the skin released from his knee, she plummeted to the ground, splattering the blood from the floor onto Rick's face.

"Sorry, baby."

Linda felt the weight of her blood-soaked hoodie when she rose. Realizing the weighted hoodie would only add to her exhaustion, she pulled it over her head and whipped it across the shed. The impact against the far wall made for a loud splat. Between the exhaustion of pulling his skin and the weight of his blood, she was a mess of sweat. She hesitated for only a brief moment before savagely stripping down to her naked form. Her husband, meanwhile, was unrecognizable. Thick hide flaps hung from his raw exposed tissue.

Another hour of tugging and tearing passed before the right and left legs were peeled of skin. Exhausted, she fell to the floor and grasped his swinging torso with both arms. She felt his cold, shriveled dehydrated skin graze against her nipples, and cried to realize he would never again make love to her.

After so many hours of pulling, her forearms ached and burned as if she'd been arm-wrestling demons. Her limbs and heart felt heavy. She took a quick look at the clock above the wooden doors: it was ten pm. She curled up into the warm coagulated blood beneath him, closed her eyes, and fell asleep.

She hadn't been asleep long when she jolted from her slumber and looked around. Her eyes immediately met Rick's bloated, grey cheeks and sunken face and she screamed as her legs shuffled against the floor to back away from him.

Coming down from the profoundly startling moment, she steadied herself and went back to work. This time, she had to run the blade back over his groin to rip skin from the crotch region and over his iliac crest. The smell of iron was overwhelming.

His inside-out skin flaps from his toes to his hips hung like drapes over his torso. Grasping the flaps on each side of his hips, she lifted her legs from the floor to give this particular pull all of her body weight. The skin did not budge. She hung onto him for a few moments and dangled with him there until suddenly, the thick fat tore with a loud snap and she was shifted violently towards the Earth.

When the skin finally gave, his intestines projected from his stomach and smacked along with her onto the concrete. Some of his internal organs fell into her bare lap. She grabbed up the sticky, thick mess to free herself then looked around for the scalpel to snip his intestines from his body so she would have room to proceed. The hardest part was over.

As it approached dawn, she had already repeated the muscle and fat removing procedure to both his arms. His face was no longer visible for the mass blanket of dermis that hung from him. The skinning was almost complete. Naked and covered in blood and sweat, Linda crept under his hide afghan to cut around his throat. She didn't want to risk damaging the face, or all of this would have been for nothing.

She braced his puckered (and hardly recognizable) face to make a long mass incision around his neck and up through the back of his skull. The trick was to yank the skin from his cranium off like a tight sock so she could slip his lower sheathing off with ease. Completing the final long incision, she grabbed his scalp. There was a long suction noise from his tissue being pulled off of the skull and then, just like a tight sock, the skin was completely freed.

She was now staring at teeth, raw facial muscles, eyeballs and fully exposed sockets with his skull dressing in her right hand in one piece. His face looked like something from her biology books in college. Carefully, she laid his cranium skin on the floor beside her before ripping clean the last of his skin suit from his dead body.

The suit plopped to the ground. He was now thoroughly skinned. The skin lay there beneath his exposed skull that shined like porcelain in the light. She looked him over and spoke to him in a whisper, "Almost there, baby."

It was time to shower and get decent sleep in preparation for what was ahead. His cast molding was going to take a lot of work, and Linda worried she may even have to go into town. Her feet stuck to the floor as she stepped over to the far wall to scoop up his oversized Carhart. Putting it on, she started for the wooden doors and shielded her eyes from the sunrise. After slamming the heavy, wooden doors shut, she scurried quickly into the house, leaving a trail of bloody footprints all the way down the hall and sticking a bit with each step. When she flicked on the bathroom light, she jumped at the sight of her reflection in the mirror.

She swallowed hard to collect herself, and let the jacket fall to the floor. Her naked body wore the drippings and traces of her husband's insides. With a shudder, she took a deep breath as she rubbed her hand across her navel. Raising that hand to her mouth, she sucked the blood clean from her fingers. She closed her eyes tight and relished the taste.

Ladies and gentlemen, we are gathered here today to witness the uniting of Richard and Linda. On this day you will witness them pledge to be by each other's side forevermore. As it says in Mark 8:10,

"And they two shall be one flesh: so then they are no more two, but one flesh."

PIECES OF MADNESS

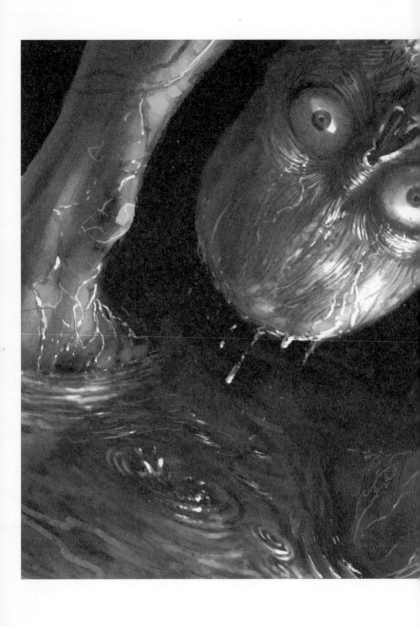

HIS MAJESTY PART II

Was Linda obsessed with Rick or with an idea?

The idea was what she saw in the picture frames surrounding her; if her home was a castle, she was the iron queen, steadfast in her ideas and what she wanted. Till death do us part? That wasn't going to work for her.

Author Robert Heinlein once said, "Love is that condition in which the happiness of another person is essential to your own." Well, if that son-of-a-bitch really loved her, he wouldn't have let the illness claim him. He wouldn't have left her and the girls to be without him. He would have fought harder.

It's okay, though. We all make mistakes.

Besides, his better half would salvage what was left of the ruins of Rome. Even if it meant stuffing Caesar.

Lunacy? Love? Both are altered states of consciousness; both are dangerous.

Thin lines.

* * * *

"Shit, shit, shit!"

It was eight am, and Linda was hopping up and down trying to hoist her yoga pants around her waist. She'd been rudely awakened by the shed door slamming, and she was terrified someone had discovered her husband. Using the bedroom door frame, she propelled her body into the hallway and wood-burned the balls of her feet from scooting in them at her panicked pace. She swung open the side door and glanced through the screen…

Of course. The winds off the water blew against the shed all the time. Why should this morning be any different? She put her hand to her chest and breathed a deep sigh of relief. Blame it on good old heightened anxiety.

With a quick pivot, Linda started down the hall and for the kitchen. Although she was anxious to get to work, she kept with her morning routine. The empty coffee pot felt as if it weighed a good ten pounds. The constant tugging at human flesh the night before left her arms fatigued. While she was slowly arranging for the coffee to brew, the phone rang.

Oh, shit.

She'd completely forgotten about the girls. She turned to lift the phone from the receiver and stopped to notice the dried blood still embedded in her fingernails. Pausing for a moment, the weight of what she was doing began to set in. It really wasn't supposed to be this way.

"Hello? Hey, Mom!"

"Yes…yes."

Linda closed her eyes tight before she proposed a new plan.

"Hey listen, uh…Would you mind if the girls stayed just one more night?"

"Oh, yes! Everything's fine."

"It's just, um…well Rick is feelin' pretty spry

58

and wanted to go out for a date night..."

"Yes, I know I'm really excited."

"Yep."

"Uh huh."

"Thanks so much, Mom. Hey, can I talk to the girls?"

She looked to the ceiling as she exhaled. This had to be short and sweet. So much to do.

"Hey, my loves!"

"Yes, Daddy and I are going to have a night out."

"Yep...yep, he's feelin' much better today..."

Linda's face wore sudden, slight panic.

"Oh...um...Daddy's in the shower now, baby dolls."

She looked once more to the ceiling. A tear escaped, rolling from her cheek to the floor. She sniffled and quickly collected herself.

"Uh-huh..."Yes, I'll tell him, honey, okay?"

"I love you, too."

"Buh bye."

With her aching hands, she placed the phone back onto the wall receiver. She leaned her head against it for a moment and drew a few deep breaths. Then she straightened up, pulled her shoulders back and blinked a few times.

The clock was ticking.

Game time.

Shoving open the screen door, Linda started on her mission. The lake air blew her hair wildly like the blades of grass surrounding the rickety wood shed. The ground was a sharp, moist cold against her bare feet, quite unlike the warm, thick moisture of her husbands' insides.

Stopping for a moment in front of the shed, Linda placed her hands on the large wood block sealing its doors. She quickly shook off any remaining attachment to reality. This was the point of no return. Best to ride the wave that was her present state of insanity. After all, she was doing the best thing for her girls. She was seeing to it he kept his part of the bargain.

Firmly gripping the splintered, heavy oak, she lifted and tossed it to the side. With just a slight parting of the doors, she was hit with a heavy, eye-tearing stench. It knocked her senses so hard that her body's reaction was to turn and crouch away from it.

She placed an involuntary fist over her mouth so as not to regurgitate while the doors widened behind her. Taking a moment, she wiped her eyes and stood from her bent position. She turned slowly but still managed to startle herself at the sight of her husband's skin-stripped body.

The once fresh ruby tissue was bloated with the texture and color of a dried corn husk, swaying gently on the imbedded cold steel. With her vision still hazed from the stench, her husband's bulging, glazed eyes were in clear focus. Any further protruded and they would have fallen from his skull.

Linda stood planted into the Earth as she surveyed the sack of rot.

"Rick, where are we going?"

"We're almost there, babe! Promise!"

Rick led Linda down the narrow hall, covering her eyes with his hands. Linda reached blindly in front of her, her fingertips grazing the walls. With the success of a healthy pregnancy, thus far, the last thing she needed was to ram her eight month bump.

"Aaand STOP."

Linda abruptly ceased her waddling.

"Now, don't peek!" He lowered his hands and gleefully made his way around her like child. Having reached the doorway to their destination, he turned the knob. The door slowly fell open with a soft creak. Eager and anxious, he quickly assumed his position. Gently

grasping her auburn tresses, he drew them behind her face to clear her vision. This was the big reveal, after all. His hard work deserved the best first impression. His hands fell from her hair and rested on her waist.

"Okay...open."

Linda let out an immediate gasp. Her smile widened, taking in the intricate craftsmanship that surrounded her. A tear fell as she slowly stepped into a fully furnished baby's room. "Baby, this is amazing! I-I can't believe how beaut—WOW!"

Rick leaned against the doorway and smiled at her and she waltzed over to the cedar bassinette. It gently swayed after she gave it a slight push. "Oh my God! It even swings!"

He chuckled as she put her hands to her mouth in amazement. Turning to the monogrammed rocking chair adorned with a large satin, pink bow, she looked to him almost sheepishly, as if she had to ask for permission.

"Go on!" He motioned to the chair. "Try it out."

She bit her lower lip in anticipation, lowering herself onto the seat. Like a queen taking her throne for the first time, she closed her eyes to take in the moment. Strolling towards her, Rick grinned. She opened her eyes to look lovingly upon him as he kneeled in front of her. She pet his blonde locks, smiled, and whispered, "Thank you, baby."

Rick took her hand in his. "I love you."

Like the skin ripped clean from his anatomy, so was the life she always wanted ripped from her. Sobbing, she mourned that memory as it passed through her mind. Linda looked to the sky, searching for answers in the Heavens. He was up there somewhere. But she would see to it that as above, so below. He would be here in at least some form and her kingdom would once again be restored to glory.

Wiping the mucus that ran from her nose, she pushed her shoulders back, raised her chin, and surveyed the shed. It was time to get to work.

Rick's raw skull grazed the slabs of his hide that folded on the floor around him. Blood stained, ivory sheets laced with hair were piled onto the cold, grey concrete. Darting for the floor, she grabbed up his skin tux. His dermis spilled out over her arms as she struggled her way to the large, black workbench.

His moist skin piles splattered about the bench where she dumped them. Just as she would for any raccoon, she followed protocol. After skinning, step two was to drying the hide. A large black air compressor loomed over the work area, but Rick had installed it too high for her, and she had to jump to tag the power button. As the heavy hum filled the shed, she hopped once more to knock the hose down. It fell into Rick's integumentary folds with a heavy plop. She reached for the silver air nozzle and began to hose his skin. She looked as if she were starching taupe curtains in a fury.

"Rick, you've had this vertigo for a week now! PLEASE go see the doctor!"

Linda rubbed her husband's hunched back. His moist face loomed over the cold porcelain bowl filled with bile. Catching his breath between rounds, he rested his forehead upon his wrist. "Honey," he gulped between words, "I think you're right. I—I'm really..." He proceeded to expel and a robe-clad Linda continued to rub his back.

As Linda dried her deceased husband's casing, she shuffled them in order along the way. Like a puzzle, she was trying to figure the order of his pieces. Thirty minutes passed before she felt friction while she moved the skin sheets around. Step two was near completion.

Linda ceased spraying and took a step back from the table. The once-disheveled slabs now lay like a uniform of latex. Speaking of latex, it was time to create the model husband, so to speak. She chuckled at her own inward joke. His decomposition was soon to accelerate and she knew it. It was a race against time if she planned to use his remains as reference.

She made her way to the industrial metal cart they used for deer carcasses, rolled it across the room and parked it in front of the putrid hanging meat that was her late husband. Back to her skin display. Crouching down, she took a glance under the work table. What she found were boxes upon boxes of molding plaster. He would, of course, require a custom cast. A custom cast that required almost all of their supply.

Linda dragged two boxes from underneath the table and scooted them to the cart. A couple of industrial buckets and some paint stirrers later, the stage of creation was set. Kneeling with a paint stirrer in her hand like a maestro, she looked into his thickly glazed eyes.

"Mr. Adkins?"

Every minute in that waiting room had felt like an hour. Rick shot up from his chair only to stumble a bit. Linda caught his arm in time enough to keep him upright. He took a moment to get his bearings before making his way to Room 201.

Stepping onto the black stool, Rick began to help himself onto the cold leather exam table. Linda attempted to assist, only to be met with aggression.

"Jesus! I'm not handicapped!"

She was taken aback by his reaction. Her once slow-to-anger husband had been lashing out at her for the past week. Shrugging it off as stress, she tried to swallow the jabs in the interest of peace. Still, she was growing quite tired of this behavior. It just wasn't like him. Thank God the results had arrived. They were more than prepared to be rid of the reality at hand.

Linda was just taking a seat when Dr. Oldman entered the room. The stout, goateed doctor wore a neutral demeanor as he shook hands and greeted them. Opening the tan folder, he looked over the MRI's, then tossed the folder behind him onto a stool. He took a quick breath and drew a small flashlight from his white coat. Glancing over Rick's eyes, he asked, "Any changes in the dizziness, Mr. Adkins?"

Wincing, Rick said, "No. Still the same."

Linda leaned forward. "I personally think it's getting a bit worse—"

"LINDA!" Rick snapped, "I'm pretty sure I know how I fuckin' feel, alright?!"

Her eyes welled with tears. "But this isn't you."

Closing his eyes and feeling a fool, Rick dropped his head low. He began to cry. Dr. Oldman had returned to the folder and was jotting a few notes. Rick looked to him like a wounded animal. "Please, tell me. What's wrong with me?"

The doctor set the folder down and put his arms at his sides. "We've reviewed the scans, and found a significantly large mass in the right hemisphere of your brain. It's evident to myself and my fellow colleagues that you have brain cancer."

A little at a time, Linda added and stirred the thickening plaster. With the consistency almost to standards, the paint stirrer suddenly broke. "Well," she chuckled, "Guess that means it's ready."

She decided to start molding the feet first. Slapping clumps of clay onto the end of the cart, she couldn't help but smile. She called over her shoulder to the carcass behind her:

"I mean, building a man from the ground up is pretty commonplace for a woman nowadays, don't you think?"

Over the next three hours she added and shaped clumps upon clumps of clay. It was just past noon when she had just arrived at his pelvis. Dripping sweat and dehydrated, Linda dropped back onto her rear to take a break. The stench was getting worse. She looked to his lifeless body. The mossy green rot was spreading.

A glass of water never sounded so good. Linda pushed herself from the floor and started for the house. Shutting the shed doors behind her, she bent for the wooden block. As she did, she caught a glimpse of a police car parked just behind her van in their gravel drive.

"Shit!"

She sealed the doors and jogged to the driveway. A young, tall officer was starting up her porch stairs to the front door.

"Jim!" She called.

The officer turned and flashed a smile. "Hey, Linda! Long time, no see!"

Trotting down the steps, he made his way towards her. He went to hug her but she stopped him. "Oh, Jim, you don't wanna touch me. I'm covered in plaster."

"Pickin' up the old man's slack, eh?"

"Yeah, well, someone's got to."

They shared a chuckle before he asked, "Hey, is he up now? I just wanted to drop in and see how he's feeling."

Linda shook her head. "I'm sorry, Jim. He's been laid up all day."

"I see. I see." Officer Jim nodded. "You holdin' up, then? Where are the girls?"

She nodded while she tried to think of a reasonable response. "Well," she started, "I sent the girls to my mother-in-law's. Ya know, so they can actually be loud and be — well, kids for a while."

"Yep," he nodded approvingly. "Well, can I see what cha got goin' on in the shed? Here I thought you weren't doin' any more orders for a while."

With her mouth involuntarily dropped open, she said, "I-I can't let ya in just now."

Officer Jim crossed his arms and lowered his brows inquisitively.

Linda continued, "I have a fan goin' in there to dry the deer hide since our air compressor went on the fritz. I wouldn't want to raise the temperature in there, ya know?"

Officer Jim simply let out an alarming, "Hmph." Linda panicked inwardly, trying to think of a response, when he said, "Well, I gotta get goin,' Mrs. Adkins. You tell your husband we're all thinkin' of you guys, down at the station."

"How sweet of you, Jim. Send the guys our love, too."

The officer gave a nod and got in his car. Linda stood and waved. She was shaking with relief, but wanted to be sure he was well out of the drive before she left the shack unguarded.

With her anxiety now reaching new heights, she turned and marched towards the side door. Time for water, a breath, and to get this casting business out of the way.

"Honey...honey?"

Linda shifted forward on the couch to gaze upon Rick's face. She shook him. He was wide-eyed and unresponsive. Frustrated, she proceeded to shake him even harder. His body merely slumped to the side towards the arm of the couch. Linda trembled in disbelief as the tears rolled. Through her clenched jaw, she mustered, "No. No you are NOT leaving me here."

She grasped his left hand and put it to her cheek. His skin felt fresh from the fridge.

He was gone.

Measuring the cast dimensions, she made sure she was as close to 5' 11" as possible. The height of the afternoon brought a half-completed cast in a shaped replica of a human's body. It also brought a further decayed Rick. Now, what to do with him?

Pushing herself from her knees, she hurried towards the far wall behind him and firmly grasped the red lever that released the hoisting chains. He fell to the ground like a bound, leaden rag doll. Hearing the cervical vertebrae snap made her cringe slightly. This once glorious product of God's engineering was now a raw pile of disgrace. Linda found herself disgusted. Not at herself. Not at her actions. But at the sight of this soulless sack of decay. She had no need for the shell; it served no further purpose. The reeking carcass had to go.

"You put on sunscreen before we left the house, right?"

Linda placed the tackle box on her lap and did a quick inventory.

Rick responded with a less-than-enthusiastic, "Yes, dear. All set." The September sun still reflected hard off these waters. Rick sat across from her at the stern of their quaint motor boat. As she toiled through the box, he rested his pale hands in a denim lap blanket. He sat with the posture of a child; slumped, exhausted, and sad. The winds blew through his oversized tan jacket as they sat in the stationary boat. Rick lowered his ballcap-adorned head and watched the light dancing on the waves.

"Linda."

She ceased her lure shuffling. With two fistfuls of colorful bobbers, her eyes set on him. Linda took in the frail state of her once well-built husband. Still taking in the beauty of the shimmering reflections off the lake, he continued.

Linda stepped over the decaying pile of tissue and bone to the far window of the shed. Just above the window was a shelf with a box of industrial-sized garbage bags. Deer entrails were disposed of in such a way. With a short jump she knocked the box from the shelf and onto the floor. It fell just inches from the jigsaw of skeleton and tainted gore. Linda bent over to be met with the foul stench head-on. She jerked back for a moment with a look of disgust. No, this was not Rick. He smelled of Old Spice and, often times, coffee. This was the smell of spoiled meat. Realizing she didn't want to vomit while gathering the remains, she started for the house where they always kept ginger pills — a seaman's best friend — on hand.

"Linda, I want to thank you."
Biting her bottom lip, her eyes began to water. In a quivering voice, she replied, "For what, honey?"
He drew a breath, still staring into the lake. He did not answer her question. Instead, he praised their surroundings "I love it out here. The peace."
She looked to the water too, to see if she could feel what he was feeling.

Linda yanked fraying tissue from Rick's bones in chunks with her gloved hands. Like pulling pork from a shoulder, she pulled at the disintegrating meat. On bent knees, she stuffed the garbage in a frenzy. It would be easier to stuff his skeletal frame into a bag separate from his flesh.

"I want to know peace again. I don't want to be afraid anymore."

"Baby, this is all going to pass" Linda reached for his chin and smiled. "You don't have to go anywhere away from us for peace. You're doing so well!"

His eyes met hers. "Oh Linda, I never want to leave you or the girls. I never would." He took her hand placed under his chin and gently kissed it.

Her brows sank as she pursed her lips like a scolded child. "Then don't."

After an hour of pulling, separating, and stuffing, two large black bags sat in the center of the shed beneath the two large, looming silver hooks. There was a coppery red stain surrounding them. Rick's body was ready for disposal. Linda peeled the gloves from her sweaty palms and threw them to the hard floor.

"Sweetheart, you know I love you...but I'm so tired."

She leaned forward and collapsed into his boney chest, sobbing. "But I need you here! You don't understand! You promised!"

Rick wrapped his arms around his devastated wife. He held her tight and pressed his lips to the crown of her head.

The shed doors swung wide when Linda kicked them open. Heaving the two bags along behind her down the grassy hillside, she made her way past the house, the girls' play set, and down to the shore line.

"No, please don't leave us!" Linda wailed into his jacket.

"Shhh, baby..." Rick pet her hair. A few moments passed as he felt her body jerk from hyperventilation.

Continuing to pet her hair, he asked if she had picked up any live bait for the trip. He felt her nose move left to right across his jacket. "Oh, no," he laughed. "We've been out here with the glow worms for so long, they're gonna catch onto us."

She looked up from his chest, her face a mess of tears. "I hate when the worms poop on my hands."

With Linda still in his arms, he threw his head back in laughter.

It took nearly a half hour to haul the hefty black bags of rot to shore, but she finally stood ankle-deep in the water. She grasped one of the bag handles with both hands and pressed her heels into the soft, watery sand. After taking a moment to build up her strength, she heaved a black bag of Rick's remains into the small, aluminum boat.

"Honey, they're just shitting dirt."

Linda scrunched up her nose in disgust and he laughed some more. He put his forehead to hers to gaze lovingly into her eyes. Then he said, "Don't let those bastards eat me, sweetie. Please. I'd rather be food for the fish out here, these majestic fish…than for some slimy insect."

When she reached two hundred yards from the shore line, Linda stopped the motor and dropped anchor. She would see to it that the man she loved got his wish. Stretching both arms out, she tried to keep her balance as she stood up carefully and peered over the boat into the deep. The cloudy gray overcast made the cold waters seem like a black, bottomless pit.

The bone-chilling winds left her face numb. Bending down, she turned back to the bags and reached both hands under the plastic. With one quick motion, she tossed a bag over the side. The violent splash nearly sent her overboard. Soaked, she fell backwards to compensate the balance.

One down, one to go.

Anxious to get the whole business over with, she grabbed the last bag up with a jerk. Once again, the violent splash toppled her over and drenched her to the core. She lay there in the puddle of water at the bottom of the rocking, freezing cold boat, staring up at the large achromatic clouds that rolled past. She whispered to the sky.

"Your wish is my command, your majesty."

Linda laughed in satisfaction there in the chilly, damp boat for a few moments more.

Now, nearly seven p.m., nightfall was upon her. The whole lake area would be engulfed in complete blackness soon. She sat up and pulled herself onto the steel seat and started up the motor. It was time to start the final step. Her vision was about to be realized.

"We're almost there."

Reaching the shore, she leapt out of the boat and pulled it onto the sand. With a wobbly march, she trudged back up the grassy hill with a newfound relief. Giddy, she decided she wanted to speak to her girls. She was so happy to give them something they could come home to.

Not exactly a father figure, but a figure of a father.

Linda practically skipped her way into the house, down the hall and into the kitchen, where she excitedly grabbed up the phone from the wall. Dialing her mother-in-law's, she twirled the cord around her fingers in anticipation.

"Hey, mom!"

"Yes...yes, we had a wonderful time!"

"Yeah, well he zonked out on me early."

"Haha, oh yeah. Definitely not used to runnin'
around like that anymore."
"Great. Me too. Say, can I tell the girls goodnight?"
"Uh-huh...Love you too."
"HEY, LOVES! Oh my gosh, I cannot wait for you
guys to come home!"
"Yes! I have a big surprise for you!"
"Yes! But you have to wait till tomorrow, OK?"
"Hey, I gotta go but I'll give Daddy kisses for you,
OK?"
"Love you too! Muuuah!"
"Goodnight, babies!"

Linda danced a few quick stomps after placing the
phone back onto the receiver, then darted out the door to
the shed. Upon entering, she took note of the current
state of the room: there was a rustic, rouge stain on the
floor alongside a long steel cart, and a long steel cart
with a gray, lumpy excuse for a lower half of a man.

The buckets in the corner were filled with mixed
plaster that had hardened. She grabbed them and made a
plan to remoisten the stirred hard mold so that it would
be pliable once again. Setting the buckets down, she
knelt to her workings of Rick's lower half. She stared at
the large space of reflective steel above her creation.

All the times she rested her head on his chest. All
those times she'd run into that safe haven. She thought
about her hands running over it when they made love.
After tying memory to feeling, she mimed her hands
around the empty space to take mental measurements.
Acting as a Michelangelo, she would build and sculpt
him to his former glory.

Now midnight, the man of plaster was realized. A
solid mannequin for Rick's skin garments. Linda stood
and turned to face the black wooden table and her
husband's dried exterior. Dead in front of her sat a long

tube of industrial strength glue. Its dispenser was a long silver gun. The swinging light bulb overhead reflected off of its shiny silver tip. Nearly punching the shelf, she quickly reached out and grabbed it. She immediately scooped up a handful of skin, starting from the skull. Quite literally grasping his face, she started back for the cart.

It was two a.m. when the mashed up mess of lumpy, glued hairy skin lay dried over a giant, hilly form. Rick's double was looking like some morbid voodoo patchwork. She figured once she picked out a great set of eyes and fashioned some teeth, it would bring life to these loose, sticky blankets of mixed up skin.

Linda stood and shuffled boxes around underneath the wooden table, looking for a tacklebox that held an array of marble animal eyes. Once it was in her sights, she managed a long reach to grasp its handle and drag it towards her. Like a girl picking out the right outfit for her dolly, so she was gleefully poking through the variety. "Brown...green. Oh, c'mon! I know there's a great shade of blue in here somewhere...AHA!"

She raised a set of cobalt-blue eyes up to the light. Piercing like they were, they were meant for a wolf. Without hesitation, she crawled back to the form and picked up the glue gun. Clumsily smearing on a large clump of glue, she smiled wide and shoved one into the right empty hole that would have been an optic socket. After gluing the second one into place, she stood up to gaze upon her work.

It was a mess of Frankenstein proportions, minus the genius. Topping it all off were the sharp, piercing... lidless blue eyes. Pure empty, soulless, and staring pupils. Seeing herself reflected in them, Linda tossed her head back to shake out her sweat-ridden and matted auburn locks. She paid no mind to the glaring one-inch difference of the eye level.

The mouth hole, just below a deflated nose, was filled with gray plaster. This simply would not do. She searched around for the scalpel she had tossed to the side, previously. The same scalpel that stripped him would now aid in sculpting him. It was time to carve some teeth.

When she found the scalpel, Linda dropped to her knees and pet the loose skin at his crown. She looked into the solid blue marbles.

"Now, smile."

Digging the scalpel across the small section of plaster, she made a horizontal line. From there she sloppily made several small vertical ones to cross it. Linda dripped sweat as she struggled to dig in, thinking about her husband's beautiful smile. Once her design was completed, it was time for some airbrush work. Taxidermy was an art, after all.

The airbrush gun was in the cellar, she remembered; Rick had colored a fish one rainy night a few months back. Housebound, she marched through the yard in the pitch black night, her kitchen light acting as beacon. Inside, she flipped on the basement light and started down the creaky wooden steps.

Deer heads, mounted to wooden plaques and covered in plastic, lined the walls. Pick-ups and unpaid orders, to be more specific. She made her way through the maze of them until she found the small motorized gun wrapped with a thin, white air tube. Next to it on the corner bench was a pack of small color bottles in a clear Ziploc baggie. As she went to grab up the small machine, she noticed a bundle of blonde fur in the corner of the workspace.

It wasn't fur, however. It was shiny and smooth. Like that of a human. It was hair.

"Oh, but it looks good on you!"

Linda tried to provide her husband with some level of confidence by buying him a wig. Raising an eyebrow to her, he cocked his head in disbelief. She couldn't help burst into laughter. "OKAY! OKAY! You can take it off!"

Rick rolled his eyes as he pulled off the shaggy platinum rug.

Linda laughed along with her husband in the memory and excitedly piled her items into her arms along with the wig. She ran up the stairs clutching the items as if she were looting.

Back in the shed, she knelt down and spread the items on the floor. It was time to paint Rick's dull plaster mouth to a pearly-white smile. Fumbling through the Ziploc, she found a pearlescent, shimmering white and raised it to the light as she loaded the gun to be sure she could see what she was doing. The soft machine's motor gave off a soft hum upon its start.

Like a maestro striking up his orchestra, she raised her hand and playfully fiddled it about before she began to paint. It didn't take too long to make a quick, thick line across the engraved form. She sat back to check her work. Linda smiled at her lipless and lidless creation. The look on the freakish face was that of a disfigured madman. She closed her eyes and sighed a satisfying sigh.

"One more thing..."

The airbrush gun clanged against the floor and echoed off the shed walls. She grabbed the wig and clenched it in her fist. She bent to the monster's face and shook it before him.

Like crowning a king, she slowly placed it onto his head. She pulled on its ends to adjust the tightness. Surprisingly, it was a sure, snug fit. Linda sat back and gazed over her creation. A horrific beauty to behold. Linda dropped her arms to her sides, raised her chin to the sky, and leaned back. She breathed the ultimate and final sigh of the night.

"It is finished."

Throwing her body forward, she lunged her body onto the morbid, disfigured creation and fell into a deep sleep almost immediately. She dreamt of a kingdom and its townspeople rejoicing in the streets. Never had she slept so peacefully as she did on that plastered form and concrete.

"Mommy! Mommy!"

The girls piled out of their grandmother's station wagon with backpacks in hand. Sue shuffled around the car to keep up with them. "Lisa! Lucy! Slow down!"

The girls stopped to look at her. Lisa looked puzzled. "Momma always comes out when we pull up."

"Honey, I'm sure your mom is putting some coffee on right now and just didn't hear us."

The girls kicked up stones on the gravel drive and they made their way to the side door. "Momma!" Lucy yelled. The house was silent yet all the lights were on.

The two girls looked at each other and shrugged.

Once Sue met up with them, she noticed an opening in the shed doors and the wooden block lying on the ground. "Linda?" Flanked by her two grandchildren, Sue marched to the shed. Slowly, she parted the doors...

* * * *

Linda Adkins was arrested on Oct 2, 2007 for hiding her husband post-mortem and was also charged with his brutal dismemberment. She pled insanity per her lawyer's advisement and is currently in prison serving a twenty-year sentence. The girls live in the custody of their grandmother, Suzanne Adkins. They are all under a therapist's care for Post-Traumatic Stress Disorder.

To this day, Linda still speaks to Rick.

Thin lines.

DOLLFACE

Pilgrim State Hospital, Brentwood, NY 1946

"Damn, it's freezing in here!"

Dr. Elias shrugged on his med coat, scooped up his clipboard, and started down the long, cold halls. Evening patient rounds weren't exactly the high point of his night. The boys down at the pool hall never got tired of the stories, though. It might be unprofessional, but scoffing at lunacy made him feel almost normal. Still, it never proved helpful when it came to getting a good night's rest.

Just five years into the field, Dr. William Elias had seen more than he ever wanted. This was hardly a hospital. More like a den for the damned: Rapists, serial murderers, cannibals...

It was the questions that kept the sheets soaked. Lying awake each night, he wondered if God had mercy on the sick mind. For their sake, Elias hoped He did. Then again...Heaven, Hell, Earth...were his patients too lost in their own dementedness to even notice a difference? In a way, he wanted to save them from themselves.

He hadn't been able to save his mother.

He remembered all too well the day she died. She couldn't take the ants crawling on her skin any longer. So much scratching, bleeding, and pus you'd think she was a leper. During the day, he'd had a nanny to care for him because his mother could not; at night, though, he was left alone. He was left alone to the sounds of his mother writhing on the wood floor. To her screams. The "ants" were the worst at night. Shortly after his tenth birthday, she finally decided she'd outsmart them.

They were going to leave and so was she.

All that was left for him was a bathtub of blood and the naked shell of the woman that bore him.

Had she been in Hell this whole time? Or did she go to Heaven as a martyr for the awful time she'd served on Earth? He didn't know how it all balanced out. If it wasn't for the distraction of his beautiful and patient wife, he might be in one of those cells, too, for all the questions that plagued him.

"Evenin,' doc." Officer Jennings tipped his cap. Jennings was the head of security and main turnkey here at the asylum. Having been Dr. Elias' right hand man for all these years, nothing fazed him. He saw these people for what they essentially were: animals. The way he figured it, they didn't need to be psychoanalyzed. Just needed a pummel from a nightstick every once in a while.

"Well, good evening, Mr. Jennings!" Dr. Elias said, thumbing through his papers. "Ready for another fun-filled night?"

Jennings chuckled. "These crazies never disappoint, I'll tell ya that!"

They started down the hall together to check up on an

old favorite, Mr. Ed Helton. Ed was committed for throwing a handful of his semen at some mothers walking their children home from school. Their screams had excited him, and he proceeded to rub his genitals through his pants in front of them. It wasn't too long before he was stomped within an inch of his life by a group of gentlemen across the street. Lucky for him, Dr. Elias convinced the judge to have Mr. Helton committed so that doctors could study the workings of his mind.

He was a rare case at the time.

"Good ol' Ed." Jennings sighed, turning the key to the heavy iron door. They stepped in to find Mr. Helton giddy like a child. He sat on his bed in anticipation and showed his rotting grin from ear to ear.

Dr. Elias knew what he was waiting for. "Well, Mr. Helton, how are we feeling tonight?"

Ed pulled on his thin, stringy hair and rocked with excitement. "Peppermint, Doc? PEPPERMINT?"

Jennings and Elias exchanged smirks.

"Yes. Yes," Dr. Elias replied. "But first, are you sleeping well? No more night terrors, hm?"

Ed emphatically shook his head no.

"Good, good," Dr. Elias went on. After scribbling on his clipboard, he reached into his white coat and shook the tin of peppermints. Ed smiled gleefully and sat upright, stretching out his hand for his reward. The instant the peppermint plopped into his hand, he shoved it in his mouth. His eyes rolled back as he savored the flavor.

Jennings laughed. "Jesus Doc, it don't take much, does it?"

Dr. Elias finished the last of his notes then bid Ed a good night. Just before they could leave, though, Ed started in. "Wait, Doc?"

The two men pivoted to face Ed. "Yes?" Elias asked.

"Well, y'see, I was wonderin' if you were a married

man, Doc."

Dr. Elias smiled. "Why yes, Ed. Happily married for almost ten years now. Why do you ask?"

Ed cocked his head before answering. "Does she let you spank her, Doc?"

Jennings drew his nightstick. "Why you little fuck—"

"STOP!" Dr. Elias put his hand on the baton. "Don't feed these perversions. It only encourages them."

Jennings sheathed his stick with disgust and they turned to leave. After the door shut, Dr. Elias attempted to break the tension. "Y'know, Lisa has been a naughty girl lately..." They exchanged a hearty laugh as they started back down the hall.

Thumbing through the log sheets on his clipboard, Dr. Elias looked puzzled. "Jennings? Do you know why this 645 doesn't have a name listed?"

Jennings smiled. "Oh, you mean Dollface? That's what we been callin' her. She don't speak a word. I think she's a mute. Quite the looker, though."

Dr. Elias skimmed through her chart. "...was found dining on a cat this morning on a woman's doorstep? My, my. This is...interesting."

Strolling up to cell 645, Dr. Elias took a peek through the small barred window. Legs dangling off of the bed, her long brown hair covered her face as she stared towards her bare feet.

Jennings opened the door, and she raised her head to face them. The doctor was taken aback by her stunning beauty. Aside from the rogue stain from breakfast that circled her mouth, she had skin of porcelain and green doe's eyes. Her raven locks rivalled Jane Russell's...

Yes, "Dollface" fit her just right.

The girl sat up straight and the hospital dress adorned her womanly curves just right. Supple breasts on the body of an angel face. She smiled and shied away at Elias' obvious trance.

He was frozen in time.

Jennings smirked and nudged Dr. Elias to break the spell. Realizing his manner, Elias cleared his throat and paged feverishly through her notes. "Uh, so... Miss...?" He began, "I believe it says here you were in fact eating a—a dead cat this morning on an elderly woman's stoop? Is that correct?"

She blinked a few times, her smile fixed. She did not respond.

Jennings snapped his fingers in her face, trying to get a rise. "Yo! Dollface! Doc's talkin' to ya!"

She scrunched her nose at him and became angry.

"Well, you can tell she just loves you, Jennings." Dr. Elias chuckled. He peered into her eyes with his penlight and studied her face for another moment. "The girl's either mute or she needs to learn some goddamn manners, that's all."

She stared at Jennings with hard disapproval; clearly she didn't care for his presence.

"Now listen here...don't you look at me like that." Jennings said. "You've got a sweet face but I ain't got no problem givin' ya a thump to the skull."

"Clear out for a minute, Jennings. You're making her uncomfortable."

Jennings' eyebrows shot up. "Are you serious, Doc?"

Dr. Elias turned his head slowly to face Jennings. "Did I stutter?"

The guard shook his head in disgust before taking his leave. "Rabid bitch."

When the iron door sounded shut, Elias glanced over the chart again. Looking up from his clipboard, he found that she'd been staring and smiling at him all the while. He smiled as he reached into his coat pocket, sounding the peppermints against the tin case. "Would you like a peppermint, Miss?"

Her look never wavered, and she didn't respond. She

just kept on smiling that smile that would bring ships in from the sea. He drew the peppermints from his coat as he walked over and sat next to her on the bed, presenting the open tin. She glanced down at it then back at him, still smiling. She was in her own happy place that no one could touch. He closed the tin and placed it back in his jacket.

When his eyes rose to meet hers once more, they locked. Lost in those oceans of jade, his heart warmed his body from the inside out. Her eyes were the only thing he could see. The smell of cinnamon and vanilla filled the room and, in spite of himself, his arms stretched out to embrace her body, her curves.

"William." She spoke softly and let out a soft moan while his hands danced over curves and felt her breasts. It seemed like just her emerald eyes were doing the talking; he never even paid attention to her lips. Her voice drugged his mind as she went on, "William...they sent me here. They sent me here...for you."

Still intoxicated from her sweet scent and swimming eyes, he responded vaguely, "Who?"

Her eyes became larger and she leaned in even closer. Staring intently into his she replied, "The ants."

All at once she stood up, grabbed his collar and hoisted him into the air with surprising strength. Dr. Elias sputtered and kicked his legs, but the panic set in when the skin on her face began to split and pus. She gritted her teeth and her head shook back and forth.

"NO! Please...DON'T!" He cried out, trying to loosen her grip from his coat. Her green eyes shrunk into red marbles and blood ran from the lacerations that appeared on her face. "Somebody please! Help me!"

She cocked her head as she breathed through her teeth. "Tell me, Dr. Elias..." Her girl's voice plummeted into the sniveling rumble of hellspawn, "DOES THIS ITCH?"

He stared in horror as her mouth dropped open and became a cavern. Hordes of black ants poured from it and rushed onto his body.

"NOOOOOOOOOOOOOOOOOOOOOOOOOO!!"

Instantly, Elias felt the crawling and biting of several armies of black ants. She dropped him to the cement, where he writhed on the floor screaming.

The iron door swung open. In flew Jennings and two female nurse aids. They dropped to their knees to restrain the screaming doctor.

"Doc! Doc!" Jennings yelled frantically. "Calm down! Whatsa matter?"

Dr. Elias screamed out, "That BITCH! She did this! THE ANTS! THEY'RE ITCHING!"

The nurses and Jennings exchanged confused, concerned glances.

"Who, doc?" Jennings asked.

Dr. Elias stopped kicking just long enough to scan the room. There was no one else there. "She did this!" he screamed. "DOLLFACE! Where are you, you cunt?"

Jennings grasped each side of the doctor's face and looked into his panicked eyes. "Listen, doc, you gotta calm down! There ain't nobody here!"

In a fit of fear and frustration, Dr. Elias pulled his legs in to kick Jennings in the chest. "Get offa me! Can't you see the ants, goddammit!?"

Jennings hit the floor just as two men in white coats rushed in to further restrain Dr. Elias. The nurses backed away when they stood the doctor up to haul him out of the room. His screams echoed off the cinderblocks.

"Poor bastard." Jennings removed his hat and hung his head. "Guess it runs in the fam."

SINS OF THE FATHER

"Yeah, I get it, we're all born sick—fallen... original sin and all that. But what do you have to do with anything!? Why do I have to tell you about anything!? I don't get it, confession. Seems to me I can talk to God on my own."

Martin was clearly struggling with religious premarital counseling. Hell, he struggled with the concept of faith in general. His case made it evident that being a Protestant man marrying a devout Catholic wasn't easy. But when he looked to his fiancé Maria, he remembered the fight he'd put up to even be seen with her. The forties weren't exactly kind to a match such as theirs: a white upstate banker had fallen for a senorita from Harlem.

His fury diminished when he caught the faint office light dance on the gold flecks in her pleading brown eyes. She spoke little English. But that squeeze on his sleeve came in clear. Martin's demeanor quickly softened and he closed his eyes in shame for his bullheadedness. He raised his hand to gently brush her long black hair from her face. She grasped it and pressed it to her cheek as Father Peters calmly defended his position.

"Martin..." he placed his glasses on his desk. "Perhaps I didn't quite explain myself to the best of my abilities."

Peters had a gentle way about him; it was one of the attributes that helped him fit the role of a spiritual leader. Well, that and he'd listened in on several of his father's premarital counseling sessions. You were either a priest or an undertaker in the Peters family. Being the charismatic man that he was, he definitely had a way with words. Talking to the dead naturally wouldn't have worked out for him.

Still, he'd fought the calling most of his life, and had even started a family with his wife, Sarah. It had been a small battle, but with some pull from his dad — who was also married — he'd been ordained into the Eastern Orthodox Church when he was no longer able to resist what he had to admit was his destiny. His faith was unshakable, and he could not rest until he had devoted his life to it.

Martin nodded solemnly, "I'm sorry, Father. That was my ol' man talking. I need to show more respect to a man o' the cloth."

"It's quite all right, Martin. But I'd like the chance better explain myself. Maybe next week?" Peters closed his Bible and gathered his notes, then stood to shake Martin's hand.

Martin shook the priest's extended hand as his other softly patted Maria's arm. Maria simply smiled at Father Peters with wide eyes of hope.

Peters spoke sweetly to her, *"No te preocupes. Él va a venir alrededor."*[1]

---

[1] Don't worry. He'll come around.

"Estoy muy agradecido!" Her eyes lit up as she turned to her fiancé. *"Y gracias por su paciencia."* [2]

Martin narrowed his eyes and smiled. "That's... good, right?"

Nodding in delighted amusement, Father Peters replied, "Yes, yes. Very good. Muy buena."

Catching a glimpse of the clock behind them, Peters jerked suddenly. "Oh my! Time flies! Well kids, we'll pick this up next week."

"Thank you, Father. And again, I—"

Father Peters put up a hand politely. "Who are we to not question, if it can bring further understanding of the Divine workings of the Father, hm?"

Martin gave an unsure nod. It was pretty evident he wasn't clear on what was just said to him.

Peters smiled. "Think nothing of it, son." As they took their leave, he called to them, "And don't worry about getting to Heaven, my friend. St. Peter knows we're trying our best to reserve your place beside the Father."

The couple stopped and turned to the priest. Martin kissed Gina's hand. "The only Heaven I believe in is the one I feel when I'm with her."

Peters stopped for a moment, then nodded. As they walked out hand in hand, he whispered to himself, "I know what you mean." He made his way down the dark, narrow halls of St. Alfred's. The sun was setting, darkening the stained glass windows around the church. The light from the clerk office acted as a beacon.

Alicia had been starting late on the church accounting. With reason, of course. Not business but pleasure. A shared pleasure. A carnal pleasure. If there was one vice a man of the cloth might have, Peters had it bad.

---

[2] I'm so grateful! ...And thank you for your patience.

Sex.

Not just sex but adultery. His father would roll over in his grave if he knew, and not just because of the glaring sin. It wasn't unheard of for a married man to be ordained in the Eastern branch, but that doesn't mean it hadn't been an uphill battle. How could this have even happened? Father Peters would pray for answers in his private chambers, but Alicia was the only one who ever responded to him about anything, it seemed. Since his wife had closed her legs, he opened up his business elsewhere.

Alicia's intellect did not match that of boys her age. Single by choice, her libido was starved. So naturally, an educated and well-spoken man was quite the turn-on for her. A twenty-something buxom blonde with rich eyes of forest hazel had lured herself Sunday's Man in Black. Meanwhile, the forty-three-year-old husband and father had enough pressure carrying the weight of a penniless church. He felt an urge to release. A primal urge.

And release he did.

Alicia looked up from her black rimmed glasses when he turned the corner. Her curls fell softly around her when she cocked her head to greet him. Although this philanderer was more constant that not, he couldn't fight the awkward altar boy inside. He stood frozen in the door as he gave a smirk and nod, as one would to a mere acquaintance. She found it cute how he'd sweat a little when she switched legs in her black pencil skirt. A ring of pearls slid around her large bosom as she exhaled to say, "I'm just about done here, John."

With that she licked her lips, spun her chair, and resumed her calculations. The furious scribbling that sounded from the pencil made Peters even antsier. He ran his hand through his slicked hair and danced his leg a bit. The tension was building like the pressure in his slacks, and a brain-drugged buzz took over watching her bite her ruby lower lip in concentration.

Suddenly, the tip of her pencil broke against the notebook. In that same instant, a maddened Peters rushed at her, spun her chair, grasped her shapely hips, and hoisted her onto the desk. Alicia welcomed the sudden onslaught of physical affection by gripping his hair. She proceeded to tongue his ear like a whispering serpent while he devoured the soft skin of her neck.

Peters' hands were roaming the broad landscape of her supple cleavage when she whispered, "Taste me." Without hesitation, he made his way to her navel, leaving a trail of kisses and soft bites. He breathed her in deeply and lifted her soft skirt hungrily.

Just outside the church, the fall winds howled loudly in the darkness, and rain beat hard against the windows. Silent flashes of intermittent lightning showcased Alicia's hair thrashing about in ecstasy. As her thighs crept closer to Peters' head, the thunder clapped harder. Reaching her climax, she involuntarily kicked her heel against the steel desk with a loud thud. So loud that the closing of the church entrance doors fell on deaf ears...

Father Peters placed his hands upon Alicia's tremoring thighs, slowly withdrawing his head from under her skirt. She was still arched in pleasure as he braced her legs to rise to his feet. Once their eyes met, she couldn't help but laugh at the glossy remnants of passion around his mouth. Realizing his appearance, he quickly drew a hanky from his pocket and wiped his face.

Alicia raised a sly rebellious brow and chuckled as she watched him struggle to regain his composure. He pressed the cloth to his mouth and muffled a prayer. With a roll of her eyes, she opened the drawer to her right to pull out a smoke. It bounced between her lips when she spoke. "Oh, would you relax, John?" Ignoring his anxious manner, she simply pointed to her unlit

cigarette and cleared her throat. He blinked a few times
before he dove into his pocket to draw a silver Ronson.
For him, these moments with Alicia began as an urgent
desire but quickly became a mess on the rug to be hid
from mother.

Wearing a steadfast poker face, he lit her cigarette.
He never wanted her to know just how deeply he felt. It
wasn't his intention, ever, to simply use her, but that's
exactly how it seemed. The truth was, his heart ached for
her. His position as a role model for his children and
congregation outweighed everything else, however.
Besides, he didn't want her falling for him. He couldn't
bear the thought of choosing which hearts to break. It
was bad enough she was calling him John. Having
housed himself inside her several times, though, he
supposed she had every right to address him informally.

With narrowed eyes, she exhaled a cloud of smoke.
There was an awkward silence setting in. Simply too
awkward for Alicia. "Come here." She stretched out her
arms as Peters sheepishly strolled over. Positioning
himself between her legs, he wrapped his arms around
her. She embraced him and rested her head on his chest.
Taking a moment, they breathed softly.

That one moment came with an eternity's worth of
thoughts. They raced through Peter's mind as he felt
Alicia slowly unfasten his belt buckle. Just as her
fingertips met his pants button, a man's voice echoed
from the chapel, "Hello?"

Their abrupt freeze was followed by a prompt
snuffing of a cigarette and a scrambled belt buckling.
Father Peters made a mad dash as Alicia hastily gathered
her books. Just across the hall was the side entrance to
the parish. Peters opened the door to find a man in a
rain-spattered, pinstriped vest and tie. His hair, although
wet, remained in its Cary Grant-esque form. He wore the
look of an anxious, fearful boy as the priest approached

him.

Peters tilted his head as he walked down the long center aisle. "Son, are you alright?"

The nervous young man looked to the floor and sniffled. He ran his fingers through his hair.

"No, Father..." He raised his head to come face to face with Peters. His piercing blue eyes were tearful as he went on, "I'm not."

Putting his arm around this broken man in sympathy, Peters asked, "My son, are you here to take confession?"

Still sniffling, the man nodded.

Just then, Alicia appeared through the doorway in a long houndstooth wrap coat. They stopped to watch her march towards the church exit. "I'll see you tomorrow, Father."

Father Peters nodded to her as he watched her open the large wooden doors, then motioned the suited stranger to the confessional. The young man walked ahead to take his place in the booth. Peters assumed his position on the other side, closed the door, took a breath, and said a silent prayer.

He waited for the rustling to cease as the man kneeled. Then the stranger spoke softly, "Bless me, Father, for I have sinned. It's been two weeks since my last confession, and I accuse myself of the following sins..."

"Proceed, son."

There was an awkward pause. After a few seconds, Father Peters lowered his brows in concern. "Go on, son. I'm listening."

A gulp of saliva sounded from the man before his shaky response. "I...I had sex with a woman who wasn't my wife."

Peters closed his eyes tightly. The telling of that sin was like a sharpened knife delivered straight to his gut. With an exhale, he resumed character and followed his memorized script. "And why did you do this, my son?"

The man wept as he confessed. "Because..." he began, "because...I could smell strawberries from her cunt."

Peters jerked in his seat. "Mind your tongue, son!"

At this, the man went on with a nervous rambling, "No, Father! You don't understand! I love strawberries!"

Peters' eyes danced from left to right listening to this vulgar lunacy. He tried to respond but was cut off by the continued outpour. "I mean, my wife doesn't like it up her ass. But-but—this broad did!"

The priest stomped his foot to silence this pervert's mouth. "That's enough!" Peters shouted. "I won't have you speaking like that in God's house!"

Silence ensued for a few moments before Peters composed himself to stick to script. "Now..." Peters began, "What are these other sins?" As soon the words escaped his mouth, he wondered if he'd regret them.

"When I banged this broad, Father, well...it was in front of her twin daughters."

Peters thought about his own twin daughters, the intense rage mounting inside him. Surely this was unforgivable and this sick individual should have residence at an asylum. Alas, it was his canonical duty to listen to this man. His hands began to shake over his mouth and he struggled to find words.

But the stranger went on, "Turns out she's married...to a priest."

When those words set in, Peters lowered his shaking, furious hands. His entire body shook. He sucked his spit through his teeth and felt his vision go black, like he was entering a tunnel. Before he could respond, the man began to laugh wildly like a hyena. A thud sounded as he fell back in the corner of the black pine booth. Confused, enraged, and out of patience, Peters kicked opened his door and violently swung open the confession box. Just as he brought his arm back to swing, however, he stopped abruptly.

What he saw was not the young man. He saw instead a tall, dark-haired man, about his age, dressed in a black suit with a goatee. Still chuckling to himself, the man rose from the corner and removed his fedora. He was brushing it off as Peters took a few steps back. Just what the hell was happening here?

The man stepped from the booth with a cocky grin, placing his hat atop his head. Looking like a handsome Mafioso, he laughed, "Pretty swell trick, huh?"

Peters' eyes widened and he backed further away from the stranger.

"And no... I didn't screw your wife."

Peters trembled where he stood, his eyes locked on this...what was he? Some deity? Of all the trips to Rome, of all the exorcism conferences, and of all the scripture warning of sorcery...nothing. Nothing could have prepared him for this moment. In his own church, no less. Could this paranormal encounter really be happening? Or was his overactive mind giving him this wild nightmare? No, he thought to himself, this is real.

With his crucifix outstretched, he solemnly announced, "In the Name and by the power of Our Lord Jesus Christ, may you be driven from the Church of God!"

The man scrunched his face. "You can't be serious!"

Readjusting his sweaty fingers around the cross, Peters continued, "We drive you from us unclean spirits, all Satanic powers, and—"

"Satan-ic powers? Pfft, I'll do one better..." With a raise of his brow, a booming crash sounded near the pulpit, and the left front pew was broken in shambles. Another eyebrow lift from this maddened force of a man and Peters watched the second row pew rise in midair before it too violently met the Earth, creating an echo that nearly shook the Virgin Mary statue from its foundation. Trembling, the priest turned back to look at the man—but it was no longer a man.

The whites of its eyes had perished. Peters was within inches of the thing's face, staring into two blackened sockets. He felt a tight grip come around his neck. Choking, he pried at the blackened fingers to no avail. Lifting him slowly from the ground, the creature lowered his voice to a pitless octave, "I am not Satanic, because I am no imitation." He hurled the priest across the church.

Peters felt his spine slam into the pulpit and his limbs numbed on impact. He dug his heels into the carpet in an attempt to sit upright. The Devil strolled up, casually dusting off his hands. "I come in here, pull a silly joke, and you insult me? Tsk, tsk. You really need to get some manners, Father."

Feeling was starting to come back to Peters' limbs but that meant he struggled to speak for the pain. "You...you said you slept with my wife."

"Well, I didn't sleep with her...BUT HEY! That's a fine lookin' high horse, pal!" The Devil smiled like a Cheshire cat. "'Cause I know sure as home that someone slept with her husband!" He tugged up his slacks to kneel on the same level with Peters, who was writhing like a wounded snake on the carpet. "Don't forget about that doll with the big tits that just left." He let out a flirtatious whistle as he offered a hand to help the priest.

Peters spurned the gesture. The God-fearing leader knew well enough to not accept help from the Devil, of all beings. With his face turned away, he whispered, "Heavenly Father, allow Your Son Jesus to come to me now through the Holy Spirit..."

Rolling his eyes, Lucifer responded, "Look, it's gonna take you a while to get up after that kick to the ass. So let me just help you. No tricks. Promise."

As Father Peters lay in humiliation, he turned his head. Now he was looking into the cool blue eyes of what would appear to be an upright man. He lay motionless, his gears moving like the flanges on a runaway train. The forefront of his mind was striving to comprehend the present situation; his subconscious, however, was silently praying for deliverance. The two of them were locked in a stare down, and Peters would not concede. He kept praying in his mind, crying silently and desperately for help. The repetition of that prayer was rudely interrupted by the demon's clamorous telepathy.

Cry out to Him like you do for her in the sack!

The shrieking disturbance taking place from within his skull startled the painfully battered Father to jump to his feet, in spite of himself. He cried out in pain, falling against the pulpit. Taking a few harsh breaths, Peters screamed, "What is it you want?"

Lucifer rose from his knees to hold his gut for hearty laughter when he watched the priest lurching about in pain. Abruptly though, he froze, ceased laughter, and dropped the smile from his face to say, "Why...I'm only here to help you feel better." He unbuttoned his suit jacket as he took a seat in the third pew—which was now the first row. "Clearly you feel terrible about your situation. I'm here to show you that you're actually not such a bad guy."

Peters exhaled and lifted his head to assume a momentary power position. "You're a liar."

"Again with the insults, Father. But I'll forgive you." He raised his head to stare Peters dead in the eyes. "See? I'm even capable of forgiveness. You and I aren't that much different. Just in our belief systems."

The priest couldn't help but listen more intently. Curiosity had gotten the best of him, and he listened to Lucifer present his case.

"No rituals or Kings in my faith," he said, motioning to the cross that hung over Peters. "Everyone's sins are innocent with the best of intentions. Some would argue that the road to my realm is paved with such." He leaned forward to add, "Which is complete horseshit."

Peters couldn't believe that he wanted him to elaborate. "What do you mean?"

"Well," Lucifer began, "I know for a fact that those who wind up residing with me know full-well what they've done. The clincher is, they do it without remorse. Whereas you, my friend... you carry this around as if you've murdered Pius. Am I correct?"

The priest did not respond. He simply hung his head in shame for allowing Lucifer to give him a catalyst to feel sorry for himself. For he knew, no matter how he put it, lust and immorality formed the foundation to his vile act of fornication.

Donning a smirk, the Devil's eyes twinkled. "Oh c'mon, Father. You're no Asmodeus."

Peter's eyes waltzed over the carpet as he took in this argument.

Lucifer adjusted his hat while he made his points. "Look, you still love your wife and never wanted to hurt her. Right? Hell, ya even hid it from everyone because you didn't want to hurt her. Am I ri—"

"SILENCE, DEMON!" Peters cried out.

Plopping his arms into his lap, Lucifer pursed his lips in faux-annoyance and used Alicia's voice, "Oh would you relax, John?" The Devil smirked as he watched the priest try to hide his shock. "She had a point, you know. Now let me make mine." He patted the seat next to him. "Come sit with me, Father."

Peters had remained silent up to this point, and he swallowed slowly before he pushed his shoulders back, faced His Enemy, and replied with a cold and simple, "No."

"Look, John. If you don't sit with me now, I gut you where you stand. Understood?"

The few beads of sweat that poured from his brow was proof enough of the sudden strike of fear in Peters. He began to take short, painful steps away from his pulpit while Satan, wearing a villainous smile, drew a toothpick and placed it in his mouth, clearly enjoying this pitiful sight.

At the end of the platform, just three steps awaited him. Slowly, Peters raised his leg to take an unsure step onto the small flight. The first step's success made him overzealous though, and with his second step he took the tumble straight onto his face. He lay there, face down on the carpet, with his legs sprawled over the stairs. Reluctantly, he raised his defeated head and looked to Satan, whose lips trembled from snickering.

"So when God doesn't help you, you look to me? Just ten minutes ago you refused my help, and asked for his...but here you are now. So, the only one of us makin' any sense tonight is evidently me!"

The priest closed his eyes and released a hefty sigh, pushing himself to commando-crawl. His feet bounced a bit as his legs slid from the steps. Lucifer impatiently folded his arms awaiting this mess of a priest to take his seat next to him. All the while, Peters' logic told him that the quicker he amused Satan and played this game, the sooner he'd be free. He just had to get through this. He'd settle his disappointment with God later.

Admiring the stained glass around the chapel, Lucifer whistled a chorus of "Chattanooga Choo Choo." Peters was unsteadily rising to his feet when Lucifer chuckled. "C'mon, Little Engine That Could!" He slapped his knee and wiped a tear from his eye for his witless comparison while the priest continued trudging towards the pew. Peters stood for a moment before him. Lucifer stopped fellating himself just long enough to turn and tap the empty space next to him.

"Now, what were we talking about? Sins, guilt... Oh yeah!" He snapped his fingers and pointed at Peters. "Yes! Why you shouldn't feel bad about stickin' it to that young slut."

A stone cold look came over the priest's face. Lowering his voice to emphasize his sincerity, he responded, "She is not a slut."

Lucifer placed his hand to his chest looking pleasantly surprised. "You see, Father?" he replied. "You even care about her! This further proves that you need not feel bad about this supposed sin."

Peters silent sigh spoke loudly of his impatience. "Get to the point."

Taken aback as if he were slightly offended, Lucifer replied, "That was the point. In fact, there were a few points in there." He shrugged his shoulders and threw his hands up to say, "I don't know how many fuckin' points you want, Father! I'm offerin' free deliverance, here! Deliverance from your guilt! Considering your unanswered deliverance plea from earlier, seems like I'm the only one offering anything around here!"

Peters buried his face into his hands. Perhaps this was a test of his faith. Perhaps he was acting as a modern day Job. Or perhaps this little game was a means to absolution by settling the score with the Divine. Whatever the reason, he was willing to ride it out if only to be free again.

Lucifer shifted and crossed his arms, taking on a new approach. "What if..." he began, "what if I told that your wife had sex with someone else, too?"

Peter's face popped up from his hands and, in spite of himself, he looked the Devil in the eye.

"Aha! Now doesn't that make it a different story? Would you not feel so bad if you wore matching stripes? Hm?"

The priest sat back against the pew, carefully weighing this potential information. "How am I to believe your word?"

Lucifer hmph'd at this. "You don't have to believe my words." He leaned over and met the priest's eyes head on. "I'll show you."

Peters watched as the church walls began to melt and drip like candle wax. The colors of the stained glass pooled together onto the floor in a sea of kaleidoscope color then reformed to reveal a room with sage floral wallpaper over a white ceramic sink. Panning around, the priest caught the familiar sight of steam rising from his bubbling Chemex. With the church out of view, he took in his new surroundings and realized...he was home.

"What are we doing here?"

Lucifer poured himself a cup of coffee and took a long sip before responding, "I told you that I'd show you proof that your wife had sex with someone else." He set the mug down firmly. "And I'm here to make good on my word, Father." He raised the checkered table cloth to dab his mouth, then scooted his chair back, rose, and motioned for the priest to follow him.

Although Peters might feel better knowing he wasn't the only one acting out of wedlock, he was now horrified at the thought of what he might be shown. He stayed glued to the chair. Looking back from halfway down the hall, Lucifer tilted his head. "John, this is for your own good. Trust me."

Peters stood and began his hobbling shuffle past his daughters' birth portraits and the gold-trimmed wall accents they'd gotten from his Turkish grandmother as a wedding gift. The bedroom door was shut and the house was silent. Lucifer grasped the brass knob, but looked at Peters before turning it. "Now listen, what I'm about to show you is a past tense stain in time. They can't hear us. Understood?"

The priest nodded to affirm, and thus commenced the longest, slowest turning of a doorknob he had ever experienced. Finally, the door fell open. There was the familiar cherry oak dresser against the wall, adorned by a large Victorian mirror — another wedding gift, this one from his mother-in-law. Its normal, still reflection was disturbed by a continuous shaking. Peters stood just behind the door frame as he watched. He feared stepping into the room, knowing what truth awaited him.

But he didn't need to enter to see the truth of what Lucifer had told of. Between the vibrations, Peters caught momentary still images of a shirtless young man, whose broad chest glistened with sweat. There also was his wife's familiar, shapely posterior raised in submission to the continuous thrusting. The mole on her lower back confirmed that what he was seeing was, in fact, his wife in bed with another man.

Before Peters could register the depths of this unnerving moment, the young man tossed his head back and looked in the mirror. He wore a schoolboy's smile of satisfaction. It was clear he was getting off on watching himself perform.

"Alright! Stop it now! I've seen enough!"

With a shrug, Lucifer obliged to bring the madness to a stop. The church mahogany walls slowly climbed back over the scene and the bottom of the dresser slipped from sight, replaced by the Church's stained glass, jewel-toned Goliath. But before the young man's face slipped from sight, he took one last glare at the mirror with his piercing blue eyes...that last second sent a panic that shot into the priest's chest. He had recognized that face as the rain-soaked man who had originally entered his confessional.

"Well, there ya have it, Father."

Peters sat and stared at Lucifer with a face as red as

the blood that flowed to it. His breath picked up watching Lucifer casually brush lint from his jacket. Having had enough of these demented games, he lunged forward and grabbed onto the Devil's left lapel. Grasping it like reigns on a wild horse, he began to pummel him.

Lucifer acted like a rag doll, limply letting the priest swing him around. Upon every burst of blood that shot from his face, he giggled like a tickled child. He fell back onto the pew as the enraged priest straddled him and reared his fist back for another onslaught. Finally, Lucifer put his hands up in surrender. "OK! OK! What's got you all riled up?"

Peters yanked the Devil's lapels to meet his face. "You said you didn't sleep with her but you did!" He burst into tears and released his grip, letting Lucifer fell back onto the pew. "WHY ARE YOU DOING THIS?" He slumped back onto his feet, grasping desperately at his hair.

But the Devil was on him. Rising to his feet in a fury, he delivered an iron clad backhand from hell straight to the priest's face. "I didn't sleep with her, you idiot."

Peters spat blood but still it oozed from his gums and onto the church carpet. Drawing the same hanky stained with Alicia's scent, he dabbed his mouth. The blood spread over the white cloth like spilled paint onto a blank canvas. There wasn't enough to catch all of it, though, and his bloody mucous streamed down his chin. "I know that was you. That was your first form when you came in here!"

At this, Lucifer threw his head back and smiled. His teeth looked like a row of alabaster stones lying in cherry preserves. "Honestly? You think I'm that good, eh?" He threw his fists into the air victoriously. "A compliment, Father! A compliment! THAT'S INCREDIBLE!" Lowering his arms, he added, "But unfortunately that wasn't me. I did not turn from one being into another."

Slowly, the priest raised his head. Now he wanted an explanation, even if he felt in his heart that he was hearing lies. Of course the Devil would lie. Then again, why would he? He squeezed his eyes shut and rubbed them with his sweating palms.

"Look, I gave you my word that I didn't sleep with your wife. And despite what my reputation might have you believe, I really didn't lie." Satan slapped his thighs before continuing, "Buuuuut... Asmodeus wanted to pull a little parlor trick on you. So we traded places. He's the one who targeted your wife—lustful demon that he is." He was in full hysterics at this point, laughing uncontrollably and wiping his eyes. "And I said, 'you're no Asmodeus.' HA! He's going to love that one."

The priest's pupils dilated. He was miles away, deciphering this mess through his anger and confusion. These feelings mounted in his chest; blood rushed to his skull and through his veins. With a face of stone, he clenched his molars, making more plasma seep through his lips.

His look was returned by a stern Lucifer. "I know you want to kill me. But I never once lied to you. And your wife did technically sleep with someone else. Now you just sit and think about that before you haul off and beat me again."

Damned if the Devil wasn't right. Father Peters crashed helplessly to his knees and wept; he was a mess of mucous, blood, and tears.

As much as Lucifer enjoyed watching anyone fall to pieces, his enjoyment was sucked clean by what seemed a swift victory. He jumped to his feet, grabbed the priest's jacket and thrashed him around on the floor. "Listen, pal! You're even-steven now! She slept with someone, you slept with someone, I didn't sleep with either of you…there's no reason either of you should be so hard on yourselves. Neither of you are destined to reside with me. Sound fair?"

The priest's eyes slowly danced their way to the floor, calculating all of this logic. There was simply no room for argument. Lucifer was right. Maybe they were even, after all, and he could seek redemption from here on out knowing their sins were parallel.

With a dramatic jerk of his arm, Lucifer raised his sleeve to check his watch. "WOW! It's getting late here, Father!" He crouched down to talk straight into Peters' ear "But listen…now that there is some sort of balance — you two are square, we're square you need to get outta here before the old lady actually does suspect something. Capiche?"

Peters nodded and slowly rose to his feet, feeling more clear-headed than he had in some time. He turned to Lucifer and asked carefully, "Did God send you?"

Lucifer put his hands in his pockets. "Nah, Father. Big man slanders me left and right in his publications. Every now and again I gotta make sure that people know that while I may be a little nuts, I'm not all that bad."

Peters nodded as he dabbed further streams of blood from his mouth. Tucking his blood soaked hanky into his pocket, he looked into Lucifer's eyes to say, "Please leave."

With that, the Devil strolled down the aisle and past the piles of pew rubble, whistling another chorus of "Chatanooga Choo Choo".

When the large oak door creaked open and slammed, a still silence took over. Peters looked around the empty church, and the night's events sank deep into his core. Even with all the damage Satan had done that evening, he couldn't deny that the events gave him a new outlook.

A broader scope. A view of the bigger picture. He was tired of beating himself up. Knowing now that balance was somewhat restored to his life, he could move forward. He now had a chance to leave behind his wrong and live a righteous life from here on.

With newfound relief and joy in his heart, Peters ran to grab his coat from the office. He snatched it from the rack and hurled himself through the halls, throwing his arms into the sleeves of his black trench as he went. The heavy doors swung open and he greeted a rainbow in the sky as the sun rose after the night's rain. Breathing in the petrochoric fragrance, he thought to himself, "New perspective. New life. Here I come."

He jogged the three blocks to his house on Grand Avenue, practically skipping up the steps once he reached his red brick bungalow. He dropped his keys for fidgeting with excitement. He couldn't wait to hold his girls and embrace his wife again. Once inside, he called out to them, "Sarah? Girls?" But there was no reply. Maybe the girls were at the neighbors. That meant...with a smile, he made a mad trek down the hall to his bedroom. He opened the door and stepped in, ready to begin again—

He didn't get to finish his thought.

Numbness overpowered him. The shock hit him like a bullet and incapacitated him. Helplessly, he hit the wood floor next to the bed; his body slumped itself against the wall. He was unable to move as he raised his eyes to a most horrific sight.

His wife, in bed with the same young schoolboyish man, was playing before him.

This time, though, he was witnessing the scene in its entirety. His wife's posterior was presented before the man, but her hands were tied behind her back. The ropey binding was sopped with blood, as were her upper thighs. She cried out in agony as Asmodeus ripped into her even further, laughing all the while. "Oh, Sarah!"

Peters cried out from the floor, "Get off of her,

demon! NOW!" A helpless Sarah could not hear or see her husband's presence. No one could. He lay there, slumped on the floor while the demon took his pleasure in this savage rape.

As Asmodeus laughed on, he threw his head back to reveal two horrified girls, the priest's twin daughters, wide-eyed against the wall. They were gagged and tied, their wrists raw from the rope's intense friction on their porcelain skin. Blood dripped onto their floral sundresses.

Lucifer appeared in the doorway. Surprisingly, Peters was relieved to see him. Now that they had established some level of trust, surely the Devil would put an end to this. In his broken state, Peters cried out to him, "PLEASE! PLEASE CALL OFF YOUR DEMON!"

With a snide smile, Lucifer just leaned against the doorframe. "Welcome to Hell, Father."

Peters shook his head in disbelief. With that, he began to cry, "No...NO! You said I was not destined for this place!"

"Wrong." Lucifer interrupted. With the sternest of demeanor, he delivered a lawyer's argument, "I told you that you were not destined to reside with me. Well, I don't live here."

He turned to leave, but the priest screamed after him, "No...NO!" he cried. "WHY ARE YOU DOING THIS!?"

Lucifer paused. "I told you that your wife slept with another, yes. Was it voluntary? No. But you didn't look at that. You saw what you wanted to see, and you felt better about it, didn't you?"

He walked away then, calling casually and coldly over his shoulder, "Next time, you might want to look at the whole scene before simply going on a mere glimpse...but there won't be a next time. You belong here, Peters."

KASEY PIERCE

"Do not be deceived, God is not mocked; for whatever a man sows, this he will also reap."

-Galatians 6:7

ADDITIONAL STORIES EXLUSIVE TO THIS EDITION

STEINER AND HOLMES
(SINS OF THE FATHER PART II)

"Miss Hays, do you remember anything else about this man? Something suggestive he may have said? Anything kinda off about him?"

Alicia sat on the cold, damp stoop of the Flushing #9 apartment building and told her story. The detectives' dense stares kept her from noticing the wet pebbles of cracked cement embedding themselves into the backs of her thighs.

She pulled her black skirt down over her knees and let out a soft *umm*. Although they hadn't even skimmed the surface of the secret affair between her and Father Peters, she felt her shame exposed. A mallet of judgement sounded loudly in her ears once she'd caught wind of the sudden disappearance of John and his family. Of course, after reasoning with herself, she knew there was no way she could have had anything to do with it. A random incident.

"I only remember that he seemed shaky," she responded. "Almost nervous about the sins he was going to confess."

Detectives Rivers and Mills exchanged less-than-enthused looks as she shrugged and added "I mean, that's what it seemed like, anyway."

Rivers adjusted his trench lapels over his broad build. He looked to the sky and quickly pondered what there was left to say. Mills filled in the blanks for him. "Well, sweetheart," he reached inside of his dingy suit jacket for his card. "Give us a call if you should remember anything else."

"Of course." She flashed a pageant smile. Her aim was to romanticize her image into an innocent girl working for the parish. But it was all an insincere mask and she knew that.

Alicia never actually loved Peters. She knew that, too. Heaven forbid she'd ask herself what possessed her to become the girl who got high from spilling semen on holy ground. She might see her reflection and discover who she really was. No one wants to see a real life monster. Alicia's intentions made her one. Hell, Peters wore blinders to keep from seeing that himself. He wasn't going to call a kettle black, is all.

Remaining regal in her manner, she gave a gentle wave to the car as the detectives drove away. Once out of sight, she trotted up the steps to her mother's apartment. She needed to take shelter, quickly. *Shelter from what?* She pondered this as she fumbled for her keys and they fell before the door.

"Alicia."

In that instant, she was an inmate snatched up and made to face the warden. An electric jolt from her heels yanked her upright and at attention. Alicia's mother was far from any prison head, though.

"Is everything, alright?" her mother asked, placing a calm hand on her daughter's wrist. Roberta was a soft woman; a gentle face you'd find in a Courbet painting.

Her blonde hair and hazel eyes made Alicia a carbon copy. Incidentally, so did the habit of running from the truth.

"Yes. Why wouldn't it be?"

"Well, mercy, Omar Bradley," she laughed. "Get in here."

In Bradley-fashion, Alicia wished she could just march to her room. But she knew her mother, like most mothers, would want to ease her daughter's troubled mind. Well, that and the aching need-to-know details of current looming drama that human beings love so much. Alicia sank into the kitchen chair and watched her mother put the kettle on. It was like a scene from a play. Someone playing the model mother.

The pleasantries between them had only become common these past two years. Her father had left them the year before that. When he walked out that door, he left broken bottles, black eyes, and the daughter he'd molested until she was fifteen. Roberta wasn't a good mother but she tried her damnedest to make sure the church didn't know that.

A good mother would have sought help. A good mother wouldn't have treated the violation of her daughter like a passing phase. A good mother would have killed the man.

"Honey, I know this whole thing has you very distraught," Roberta said over the click of saucers. "I'm worried myself." She turned to Alicia and released a sigh of sympathy. "I know he was a decent father figure to you."

At that, Alicia simply pursed her lips, looked to the floor tiles, and nodded. Christ, that was the last way she wanted to think of him. *His* hands had been welcome on her breasts, after all.

Roberta set the teacup before her. Alicia bobbed the bag and thought of her grandmother, the only person who made her feel safe during troubled times. Growing up, after school drop-ins became Bible lessons that pertained to anything she was feeling at the time. Sad, scared, anxious... Grandmother had a verse or hymn to remedy it.

There was one verse Alicia kept in her back pocket, Luke chapter ten, verse nineteen. She armed her psyche with it whenever she was feeling powerless, like today: *And I have given you authority over all the power of the enemy, and to walk among serpents and scorpions and to crush them. Nothing shall injure you.*

That verse was her shield. When she heard her father stumble in the door from Frank's Pub, she'd repeat it as one would Hail Mary. It may have been placebo. But sometimes the shield seemed to work.

She closed her eyes and breathed in hints of rose from the tea brewing in front of her. Feeling for the bag's string, her hands met a hairy and rigged texture; a small, thick branch that curved between her fingers. Her eyes snapped open and she raised the bag to her face, finding herself within an inch of a clawed arachnid. The mucousy haze over the insect's beady eyes penetrated hers. Angered, it snipped at her.

Alicia screamed as the tea bag fell from her hands and splashed into the scalding water. Her mother grasped her shoulders to cease her thrashing.

"What?" Roberta cried. "What's wrong, honey?"

"Scorpion!" Alicia screamed "In the tea!"

Roberta looked to the cup and the sopping mess around it. She saw nothing but the bag, cup and saucer, and a soaked wooden table.

"There's nothing there, dear." Roberta pet Alicia's hair as the girl caught her breath. "*Shh...* There's nothing there," she whispered. "Nothing at all. Your nerves have you all wound up."

Roberta pressed the crown of her daughter's head to

her chest. Alicia's breathing slowed.

No shelter here. No shelter out there. What she feared seemed to be housed in her mind. *Why am I so on edge? she asked herself. What am I scared of? That I'll disappear too? That our affair will get out? With eyes pressed tight, she lied to herself: It never happened. None of it. If I say it didn't, it didn't. He's gone anyway. Never coming back.* She opened her eyes and nodded in agreement with her delusions.

"Feeling better?" Roberta asked. She gently moved Alicia's hair back to look upon her face.

"Yes, much better. I...I don't know what that was about."

Her mother chuckled, "Oh, your mind will play tricks when it's heavy." She grabbed a rag for the mess. "Dear, I don't think its tea you need."

The wooden stool groaned against the floor as she pushed it in place to reach above the cabinet. Alicia was pulling her messy blonde mop behind her ears when she heard the chime of a few coins.

"I think a milkshake is the snake oil cure for your ailments."

Alicia smiled as her mother placed the coins in her palm. *Maybe she's right*, she thought. *I just need to treat myself and press on as normal. This will pass.*

"Are you coming?" Alicia asked.

Her mother was dabbing the sopped table. "Oh, no." she said. "I have to work a nap in somewhere, or I'll fall asleep during tonight's mass. I haven't been to St. Augustine's but I hear Father Joseph speaks slower than molasses on a winter's day."

They laughed together and in that moment, Alicia could shake off the fear she'd felt from imagining the scorpion. She must have imagined it. She'd been through worse things, real things with her mother. She could get through this.

Feeling lighter now, the breeze seemed to pick her up as she walked down the street, bound for Duggert's Diner. The dampened cement was drying up, though her saddle shoes made prints from the previous rain. She took in the beauty of the afternoon's evening disguise, with its silvery overcast. The clouds picked up speed and by the time she took at the corner of Steiner and Holmes, the street was draped in darkness.

Of course I didn't bring the umbrella.

The leaves scattered from the sidewalk, and then the cement itself disappeared. The city's noise abruptly turned to deafening silence. Alicia looked about her, trying to make sense of her now-gone surroundings, but even her hands and feet had disappeared from view. The wind had stopped, the air was cold, and dead space had her surrounded.

It was just black.

Fear set her instincts to run; to turn back. But before she darted into the dense nothingness behind her, she saw a dim light up ahead. The light you'd see from a lamp. Instinctively, she ran for the warmth of the light. The blackness became rows of floral wallpaper; the cement, wooden planks.

Alicia slowed, catching her breath. *Did...Did I just walk into someone's house?*

She tiptoed around a neatly made, quilted bed and cherry wood dresser. Any other person would be nervous about trespassing but her dreamlike state of consciousness released her from any trace of fear. There were portraits of an elderly couple and of two children she'd seen at the church. Two girls with matching features; faces of porcelain and blonde ponytails. The picture just to the right of them—Alicia tumbled back. It was a portrait of a young Father Peters and his wife at his Eastern Rite of Ordination.

I'm having a nightmare, she thought.

She ran through the hallway plastered with a gallery of Peters' family pictures. She fled through the kitchen. A whistling tea kettle startled her and she ran even more quickly to cross the living area's sienna carpeting. *The door*! She leapt towards the knob and yanked the oak door open.

No porch. No walkway. Nothing but the cement at the corner of Steiner and Holmes.

She was back where she started. Slowly turning a complete 360 degrees, she checked to see if the sidewalk and shrubbery that surround her was, in fact, real. It was. Even the traffic sounds had resumed. She sighed and pressed her palm to her forehead, *What's wrong with me?*

Stretching her neck and shaking her arms about, Alicia tried to get in touch with the moment, with reality. She had little choice but to chalk it up to irrational lunacy, and with a deep breath she resumed her trek to the diner.

Once she turned that corner, darkness swallowed her surroundings yet again. The honks and brake squeals turned into soft wooden floor creeks and she was back in John's marital lair. She stood just before the door frame, refusing to enter. Her palms began to itch and she scratched them nervously. What was she to do?

She stared blankly, trying to organize her thoughts. That's when the crackling began. A noise that crept, as did its source. Straight ahead, in the small opening of the top dresser drawer, two small pinchers arose. The crackling of the scorpion's exoskeleton became louder as it struggled wildly to escape.

Then a tapping chorus sounded from beneath the bed. An Exodus plague of scorpions rushed into plain sight. Waves of rigged tails topped with stingers rushed over the floor. Alicia fell back into the hall and her scream drowned the hundreds of pincher-armed dancers.

Her path through the house was orchestrated just as the last: the startling whistle from the kitchen, the carpeted obstacle course through the living room, and the jerk and loud whine of the heavy wooden door.

She stood and wept helplessly at the corner of Steiner and Holmes. A few steps backwards, and everything disappeared again. She was deserted here, in this corner housed in a black sea. This was madness. With palms pressed to her eyes, she stumbled about for several steps.

And then she bumped into a person. Her eyes stung when she opened them, but she clearly saw the man standing before her, wearing a black suit and warm smile. A stranger, but at that moment she felt him her Savior. Hell, it could have been just about anyone, just to know she wasn't alone. It was a sign of life outside this dimensional prison, and another being. That was good enough for her.

"Are you alright, Miss?" The man took a hard look at her.

A smile surfaced from the mess of damp flesh that was her face. "I am now," she said. "God, I'm so happy to see you!"

He chuckled heartily, saying "God I am not. But maybe I can be of assistance?"

Alicia raised her hands to ready her presentation of her current scenario. Hesitating, she struggled to put into words what she'd just experienced. "I...uh..." She took a few breaths, then became frustrated. "Listen...I was walking down the street, but I keep walking into someone's house—only I'm not intentionally going in the house. I mean, I know the guy—knew him... and um..."

The man narrowed his eyes.

"Look, I know I sound crazy. But when I walk a few steps, everything becomes dark and I'm in my old friend's room. *Gah!*" She threw her hands into the air, frustrated, certain that she sounded completely crazy. Was she?

The tall, dark stranger placed his hands in his pockets. "I don't think you're crazy, doll. I think you're just having a hard time. Can you show me what you're talking about? I'll walk with you, *hm*?"

Alicia was stunned he was even still standing there listening to her lunacy. Such a godsend. She let out a relieved laugh and said, "Yes! But I just hope it happens again so I'm not—well…maybe I hope it doesn't."

He drew a comb from his pocket and ran it through his slicked hair. "Okay, crazy lady." He licked his lips a bit as he lined up the sides of his do. "If I'm going to someone's house I've never met, it would be rude to look unpresentable."

Faced with this stranger and his smug, charming antics, Alicia forgot herself, her predicament, for just a moment, and threw her head back in laughter. But the moment was broken by the thought of the scorpions. She snapped back to attention, fully aware that she may actually be going insane.

He linked arms with her and smiled. "Ready?"

"No." she replied looking into the distance that would soon fade from sight. "There were scorpions in the room last time."

"Scorpions?" He repeated the word to make sure he heard her correctly. "Like the desert bugs with stingers and whatnot?"

She nodded shamefully. "But that could have been make believe too. Listen—" she gripped his sleeve as he leaned in closer. "If this doesn't work and you don't see what I see, please don't have me committed. I'm all my mother has."

He put a soft hand under her chin and looked into her hazel eyes. "Honey, if this doesn't work, I've never seen this stunning face. Okay?"

Feeling calmed and charmed all at once, she smiled and nodded.

They took a few paces, arm and arm. And then the street sounds were abruptly cut as if a metaphysical iron door had shut behind them, and darkness ensued. Much to Alicia's surprise, the man *ooh-ed* like a cynic in a haunted house. It was clear he wasn't scared. Still, she pressed on with him until they reached the wood hallway floor just before the bedroom.

He skipped forward and poked his head in. "Hello? Any scorpions in here?"

She followed him cautiously. *This man is just as nuts as me*, she thought.

Suddenly, he dove to the floor. He pantomimed a horn and squeezed it under the bed. "HONK! HONK! Come out, you deadly bastards!"

Alicia studied him, her suspicion rapidly turning to fear. "Wha...What are you doing, mister?"

"Why, I'm securing the room, doll," he said, with a toss of his hands to the walls around him. He snapped his fingers. "Ah. I know the trick. Watch this." He closed his eyes and cleared his throat. Crossing his hands in front of him, he looked like a minister about to lead a congregation in prayer.

"Inscendo."

Alicia didn't understand the word, and just stared at him quizzically. That's when she saw a set of claws rising its way up to his shirt collar. She threw her body into the wall behind her, watching as it grazed its pinchers over the man's lips. He giggled at the tickle. The shock of the moment choked her.

He opened his eyes and gave her an endearing look.

"Alicia..." he began. "I'm so happy to give you this."

"Give me what? How...how do you know my name?"

He ignored her questions. "Many people don't get the

chance to conquer their fears." He reached into his shirt and grasped the large arachnid with his hand. It did not pinch him or strike him, but sat peacefully in his palm.

Alicia ran.

Down the hall, past the boiling whistle of the kettle, across the living room, and through the door. Her quick rationalization told her to just keep running once her feet hit the cement at Steiner and Holmes. But she met him again in that same room, in the same moment, holding a large creeping scorpion in his hand. In stopping herself short, she fell onto her back. She scooted herself against the wall to back away from this display. The same place Father Peters fell to watch the repetitive savage rape of his wife.

As Alicia gazed at the stranger in terror, backing herself further up against the wall, a man's screaming caught her attention. She looked over to see John trapped next to her and crying hysterically.

"John!"

But he could not hear. He went on crying at the horrific sight before him. She followed his eyes to the vision before him: his two twin girls bound with bloody rope, watching the horror show of a man raping their mother. John had been trapped in this moment for just shy of an eternity, already.

Alicia closed her eyes tight and screamed, praying this mirage would leave. But when she opened them, there the man was, crouched down, face to face with her, dangling the now riled and savage insect.

"Why are you doing this?" she screamed, thrashing her head about.

"Because I have a gift for you, Alicia!" he said, his voice like a boisterous announcement. "Christ gives you the power to crush scorpions? Nothing will injure you?" He threw the scorpion behind him and shouted so that he spat in her face through his speech "No one can injure you if you *are* the scorpion! No need to run if others run from you!"

He grasped her face tightly between his hands and squeezed her thrashing head, forcing her to stay still. "You're halfway there, Alicia! You stung this man! You ate his seed! Didn't you?"

She shook her head, her eyes squeezed shut again.

"DIDN'T YOU, ALICIA?"

He shoved her head to the right. "Look at him... Look at your man! He suffers now! Paralyze him! Take away his pain!" He jerked her face back to his own and said softly, "Inscendo."

Her irises, once an alluring forest green, were now molten swirls of black glass blown by the soon hellish hereafter. Eyes from glass to slate stone, she rose from the floor.

He backed away from her to watch the unholy transformation, licking his lips at the loud snaps and the sound of flesh tearing. Glistening yellow legs sprouted from each side of Alicia's bleeding chest cavity. The legs lifted her and she cried out in blinding pain, her torso stretched beyond any human capacity.

The man looked up at her in awe of his creation. "Ultimate power, Alicia! Can you feel it?"

She couldn't answer for the blood and thin watery spinal fluid pouring into her mouth from her severed column. Her arms hardened into yellow husk-like hooks and grew to gargantuan proportions. He watched her mutilation gleefully, dancing his hands on the air like a sadistic choir conductor. Once her head touched the ceiling, he slammed his right hand down against the air as if ending a thunderous sonata.

Alicia's body tipped and her eight legs met the floor. She was now a mess of torn human flesh and strong yellow exoskeleton. Her head was still attached but simply hung to the side, mouth gaping. She was brain dead. He studied her slackened face for a moment, then struck up the chorus once more to make way for a large furry branch to tear through her anus and rise above her head. Her body shook as the stinger barreled its way out of the back end of her flesh. Her sheer size filled the room and he giggled happily to be forced to the corner. He let out a sharp whistle to Father Peters, merging their dimensions.

The priest heard the whistle and his eyes snapped upwards to see the towering monster before him. His blood rushed through his veins like ground marble and he screamed.

"I've brought you some mercy, my friend," the dark stranger called to him. "Courtesy of an old friend!"

Alicia's enscorpioned carcass brought its tail back and plunged the stinger through Peters' head and neck with brute force. His body shook violently for a moment and then ceased, though he still hung there, impaled. He went stiff. Paralyzed. Her gaping mouth widened and slobbered like a drunk glutton. She ingested him slowly, starting from his head and working her way past his shoulders. The sounds of her clicking and sucking filled the room, and then she was finished.

Alicia's eyes shifted to the horrified and screaming children.

They were next.

PM 881

TIME: 2:30

M
45

CARA-MIA

JAY AND THE AMERICANS

CARA MIA

Florence, KY 1965

"Phil, honey, it's on!"

Phillip Clemens shuffled his dumpy build into the living room in a hurry. Nearly doing a belly flop onto the shag carpeting, he dove for the TV dial. Although a young man of sixteen, he squealed like a boy of seven in his striped pajamas. Doctors said his mental acumen was "lacking." And there was the stutter. But he took the love his parents gave him and spread it about. Despite having the build of a defenseman, he had little interest in sports. Instead, the thought of excelling at academics excited him. That, and Rock 'n' Roll. The kid lost sleep pantomiming his best Frankie Valli in the mirror.

Jay and the Americans were playing Bandstand tonight. Oh, he never missed an episode. With fists to chin, he kicked his legs about in anticipation. His mother smiled from behind the couch in her paisley apron and well-kept blonde bouffant. Phillip was always very observant. He took note of every single detail, wherever

125

he was. Captivated from the moment the stage lights lit up, he watched Jay and the boys take their places. Slicked hair and black cardigans set the tone for this class act. The girls screamed for Jay before he even opened his mouth to belt in operatic fashion, "CARA MIIIIAAAA why...must we say goodbye?" Phil stared intently at the screen, his eyes glazed over. He was caught up in the moment. Caught up in the music. Caught up in thoughts of Cara Miller.

Of course, most boys got lost in thoughts about the captain of the Bellmont Cheer team. The way she pressed her books to her chest... The blonde ponytail that swung about... No Bellmont boy could shake the image of her pouty lips and hypnotic doe eyes. Of course, the only kid armed with enough foolish pride and a sack of brass asked her to be his girl: Johnny Black. Son of wealthy landowner Buford Black, it was ingrained in him to be the best, bang the best, and don't you be late for church.

He may not have been sharp, but Phil was sensitive to those around him. Cara's sadness made the air dense. There was no denying it. Often times, he'd see her cry in the passenger seat as Johnny peeled off in his red pickup after school. If she wasn't puttin' out, she was gettin' out. That was his motto. Students stared but quickly moved on. No one wanted to tangle with that mess. Phil's heart broke for her.

Jay snapped along, keeping rhythm while the girls screamed. A handsome romantic with class; a shining example of everything Phil wanted to be for Cara. When the final beat hit, Phil shot up and clapped frantically.

His mother, Gladys, lit a cigarette and chuckled. "Boy, you and that rock 'n' roll."

Phil turned to her from his knees. "Momma, I want to enter the talent show at school! You-you-you think I got a shot?"

Gladys cocked her head as she withdrew the lit cig from her mouth. "Of course, darlin!' You sing just as perdy as a whippoorwill!" She nodded to the television. "Better than ol' city boy, up 'ere."

Phil licked his lips as his mouth widened into a grin. Surely he would win Cara's heart with Jay's hit song. It had her name in it, after all.

The next morning, Phil sailed through the halls of Bellmont eager to reach the office. His excitement was best told by his tan button-up being a mess of mismatched buttons. Finally reaching the office door, he barreled his way past Secretary Milton's desk.

"Slow down, son! Where's the fire?"

Phil stopped to place his hands on his knees and catch his breath. "Gee, I-I-I'm real sorry 'bout that, Mrs. Milton. I j-j-just wanna sign up for the talent sh-sh-sh-show."

Mrs. Milton put on her black rimmed glasses and shuffled papers about her desk. "Of course, Phil. Let me just find it here. Whatcha doin' for us, anyhow?"

"I'mma gon' sing you a lil r-r-rock 'n' roll, ma'am!"

Mrs. Milton smiled as she placed the numbered sheet with a pencil before him. "Well, well! That sounds mighty fine, Phil. I sure am lookin' forward to it."

Phil's tongue danced around his lips as he clumsily signed his name.

"Now, you know you gotta be backstage at five thirty 'cause the show's gonna start at six sharp, ya hear?"

Phil nodded emphatically as he stood up from signing the paper.

"OK, honey. Now you run along before you're late for homeroom."

Phil nodded emphatically once more, still standing there at her desk.

She raised an eyebrow. "Well go on! Shoo, boy!"

Phil wound up and barreled his way back through the

door as Mrs. Milton chuckled to herself. "He sure is a corker."

He swung open the glass paned door during roll call. The class shot their attention to him, as did Mr. Keefe. Lowering his glasses, he smirked in his navy cardigan. "Glad you could join us, Mr. Clemens. Take your seat."

Breathing heavily, Phil scooted his way behind a row of students. He couldn't help but bump their chairs for his size. After a few sighs from the row, he had reached his seat next to Lisa Cooper; a raven-haired mod who didn't quite fit the small town mold. Her jet black bob, thick eyeliner, and cryptic silence left her with few friends. That was just fine with her. But with her vast intellect and short patience, nothing annoyed her more than having to sit next to Phil every morning. Being the polite, cheery fellow he was, he tried anything just to get her to talk. He always put his best efforts forward to making new friends. Clearly annoyed, she fidgeted and grasped her oversized heart locket.

Phil stared at Lisa's small stack of books. One was a small black notebook bound by a leather belt. He noticed the cover was blank. He pointed to it. "What's that?"

Lisa rolled her eyes. "A book."

Even Phil could sense her annoyance. Still, he sheepishly proceeded, "Wha-wha-what kinda book?"

She closed her eyes and sighed, "Poems. They're my poems."

Phil smiled. "Like Jack K-K-K-K..."

"Kerouac?"

Phil snapped his fingers. "That's it!"

Lisa couldn't help but smile. "Well, well, Phil. Guess you ain't a square after all."

Phil blushed when Lisa laughed.

Mr. Keefe peered over his glasses at the announcements in front of him. "Now y'all remember the talent show is this Friday. So please don't ferget 'bout that. Lunch today will be meatloaf and …"

Phil whispered to Lisa, "I'mma gon' be in the talent show."

Lisa nodded approvingly. "Far out! What are you doing?"

"Well, d-d-don't tell anyone but I'mma gonna sang 'Cara Mia' for Miss Miller."

"Cara Miller? The cheer captain?"

Phil nodded.

Lisa's smiled faded and she turned to stare at a blank chalk board. "God help you, boy."

The school day went like any other. Phil ate his lunch outside on the picnic bench with some nerds from yearbook club. Their jock jokes brought him to tears. But Phil became quiet when he noticed the red pickup go by. Johnny and Cara were coming back from lunch. Cara rested her elbow on the window, looking out like a scolded puppy. She looked miserable. Phil sat up straight like a knight embarking on a quest. He would be the victor on Friday. He knew it.

Phil bobbed and hummed on the bus home from school. He daydreamed about stealing the talent show. Apparently, the humming was annoying Tom Armstead who sat just in front of him. Tom was one of Johnny's goons and the Bellmont kicker. He stood up on the seat, spun quickly to Phil and smacked him atop his head. "Shut up, stupid kid!"

Phil cowered. As often as he was teased, he tried his best to shrug it. He was a tender young man, and retaliation was not in his nature. Instead of decking Tom, he sat solemnly with quivering lips. The rest of the students just snickered at this.

Phil was silent until the bus pulled alongside his house. There his mother stood beside the mailbox on the gravel drive. In a green mini-dress and Dusty Springfield do, she awaited her son. He smiled at her through the window and waved. Gladys watched him move down the aisle towards the door, and she witnessed him take a dive. The moment was followed up by laughter from the students.

In a fury, she marched through the open bus doors and up the steps. She rushed to help her son when Tom looked down to say, "Don't worry, Mrs. Clemens. He had a nice trip."

Gladys helped Phil stand up and pointed her finger in Tom's face. "Now you listen here, Tom Armstead! My son ain't no one to tease err bully!"

Tom started to speak but she interrupted, "Shut up! Just 'cause you're mad everyone knows 'bout your daddy and them whores don't mean you gotta take it out on ever'body else!"

Tom was left speechless and ashamed while she marched her son off the bus. The students sat in eerie silence, as did the bus driver (who had no objections to Gladys serving up justice.) Once they had stepped off the bus, the students glared silently at Tom, who was on the verge of tears.

"What?" he shouted. "Mind ya own business!"

Hastily trudging up the gravel drive, Gladys linked arms with her son. "Never you mind them lil spoiled assholes, honey."

Phil bowed his head trying to hide his hurt and dismay, but his mother stopped to grasp his face. "Now you listen to me, Phillip Craig Clemens. You got a bright future ahead a'you." He nodded as she went on, "Them boys keep carryin' on like 'at, they gon' git what's comin' to 'em. I can promise you that!"

Phil's lips quivered. "I didn't do n-n-n-nothin,' Momma!"

Gladys pulled her son into her arms. "I know, darlin.' People act like'a fool when they know you're better than them. You know that, right?"

Phil nodded, smearing mucus from his nose onto her dress.

"OK, sugar. C'mon now. I gotta get these steaks on before your daddy starts a'hollerin.'"

Phil's father came through the screen door and onto their rickety porch, smiling. "There's my boy!"

Phil smiled back and waved from the drive. "Hey, Paw!"

His father, a jolly man, waved them in. "C'mon now! I'mma start lookin' like Porter Wagoner here, in a minute!"

His wife chuckled. "I dunno, Judson. Maybe that's a good thang!"

With backpack slung over his shoulder, Phil headed straight for his room once he got inside.

His father stuck his thumbs in his suspenders and called after him, "You got homework 'err, boy?"

Phil turned to face him. "Yes, Daddy."

His mother peered around the kitchen door. "NO music till you get yer homework done, ya hear?"

Judson looked at his wife once Phil had disappeared to his room. "OK. What happened?"

Gladys shook her head as she washed her hands. "The Armstead boy."

Judson plopped into his arm chair with a sigh. "Aw, piss," he muttered to himself. "These boys is gonna catch hell one'a these days."

Phil pulled out his Algebra and laid it on his writing desk. Picking up a pencil, he licked the tip before he began. Having completed only one question, he glanced over to his record player beside him. His Turtles record was just itching to be played. Phil looked behind him to a closed door then back to the player. Without further hesitation, he threw on his oversized Koss headphones. He licked his lips anxiously as he switched on the turntable. After placing the needle gently onto the shiny vinyl, he rocked and sang softly, to his own tone-deaf tune, "Go away from my windooow. Leave at your own chosen speeed..." Just as the song was about to peak at its chorus, he felt his headphones lift from his noggin. Startled, he jerked and turned. There stood his mother with pursed lips and narrowed eyes. He slumped a little. "Sorry, Momma."

Given the day's events, she just smiled and sighed, "Dinner's ready."

Just a few blocks over, Cara Miller stood on her back porch. Her evening hadn't been enjoyable at all. Her bastard beau came and played house with the family. Put on the model boyfriend act for the folks. They were easily sold on his charm and his family's money, and the idea of their daughter marrying into the Black family invalidated any opposition Cara made. They wouldn't hear it. Once she even had the courage to tell her mother about him forcing himself on her. Oddly enough, her mother brushed them off as overdramatized stories. Cara was going to carry out the plan she wished she had: marrying rich. Leave Johnny, and Cara would lose her mother's respect. God and the walls, truly, were the only ones listening.

Phil jumped into the shower before bed, chipper as ever, carrying on with a boisterous rendition of "Cara Mia." Atonal but with profound enthusiasm, nonetheless. Just one day till the big show.

The school day started as normal the next morning but had the added delight of actually chatting with Miss Cooper. Scurrying down the hall towards history class, Phil failed to notice his shoe lace dragging behind him. Just as he was about to reach Mr. Johnson's classroom, he stepped on his lace and fell to his knees. He heard some snickering when he landed, his book and folder flying away from him. When he stood to brush himself off, his items were being handed to him, and he heard a soft voice ask, "Are you OK?"

Phil reached up to retrieve his things and he saw a sweet face reminiscent of Annette Funicello. It was Cara.

He stared in awe and silence. She smiled in her red and white cheer sweater. "You best tie your shoe, boy, 'less you wanna bash your head!"

A muffled voice sounded from behind her, "He did that a long time ago!"

There was collective laughter and Phil lowered his head as he slowly took his books from her hands.

Cara whipped her ponytail around. "Shut up, Billy!"

She turned back to Phil and sighed, "Well, be careful, ya hear?"

He gave a slow nod and she left for her class. Frozen in time, he watched her bob down the hall.

A short gray haired man poked his head from Room 207. "Well, son? Time's a wastin!'"

Phil snapped from his trance. "S-s-s-sorry, Mr. Johnson!"

History was Phil's forte, if anything was. His father being a former military man himself, he found WWII very fascinating. The class was still buzzing when Phil took his seat in front and Mr. Johnson called for silence. "Quiet now and pay attention! Today is review day for the test tomorra. It is in your best interest to jot down all the fine points."

Mr. Johnson began to scribble on the board. "Now, who can tell me which of the current states was not a part of the Northwest Territory during the Civil War?"

Turning back, he scanned over the class before pointing to the school's running back, Billy Abbot. "What about you, Mr. Abbot?"

Billy threw his hands up. "Pfft. I dunno. The second one up 'err?"

Mr. Johnson sighed heavily, "No, Mr. Abbot. Not

Indiana."

Phil's hand shot up.

"Yes, Mr. Clemens?"

With shoulders back, Phil announced the answer with utmost confidence, "Iowa."

Mr. Johnson smiled. "Very good, Mr. Clemens!" He shot a look of disappointment to Billy. "I see someone don't wanna repeat this class, unlike Mr. Abbot, here."

Phil bit his lip trying not to laugh, and felt a swift kick to the back of his chair.

"Shut up, retard," Billy hissed.

The bus ride home was thankfully uneventful. When the bus pulled in front of his house, there stood his mom as always. She lit up inside from the smile on her son's face. When he had a good day, she had a good day.

That night at dinner, Phil's father asked him to pass the biscuits when his mother remembered the talent show. "Darlin,' ain't you sangin' tomorra night?"

Phil nodded, his face gleaming. He turned to his father. "Daddy, you comin' to see me?"

His father scooped mashed potatoes onto his plate. "Now you know I gotta work the late shift, son. 'Less you don' wanna eat next week."

"I know, Paw."

Judson rested his chapped and blistered hand on his son's shoulder. "Now you know I'd be front'n center if I could, boy."

"I know, Daddy."

That night, Phil could hardly sleep. At ten pm, he shot up from his bed trying to decide what would look better: if he delivered the song on one knee or stayed upright during the performance. It wasn't any better at school the next day. The very thought of standing before the student body was terrifying, let alone singing acapella. He asked Lisa if she'd come and cheer him on.

Her reply was filled with as much optimism as she

could muster, "I don't know about 'cheer,' but I'll show up. You're lucky, kid. I don't come to nothin.'"

Come five p.m., Phil was in the brown polyester suit he only wore to funerals. His mother was struggling to adjust his yellow bow-tie while he nervously bounced about.

"Now hold still, honey," she said. "You're a figidin' like your Uncle Don after they done took him off them pills."

Phil shuffled his feet against the dusty stage floor. Beads of sweat formed on his brow and he bit his lip before looking to his mother for encouragement.

Gladys combed his hair back with her long, pink fingernails. Placing one hand on his shoulder, she locked eyes with him to say, "Baby, you're gonna do just fine. God done gave you a gift, darlin.' Now it's time to show the world." With that, she placed a firm kiss on his forehead, leaving a ring of mauve. In motherly fashion, she then licked her thumb and proceeded to rub it off.

Mrs. Milton, the secretary, appeared from behind them. "We're about to start! Phillip, honey, you're number three, just after Vince Carter does his magic act."

The house lights dimmed as she rushed away, and the darkness was abruptly pierced by a spotlight on Principal Bauer. Mrs. Milton could be seen in the shadows running towards him with a microphone. The principal retrieved it and tapped on its orange foam top. He cleared his throat before shrugging to adjust his beige suit jacket.

"Uh, students..." he began nervously to a buzzing auditorium. "Now listen here. I want quiet, now. We're 'a gonna start the show, here."

Mrs. Milton rolled her eyes. She stomped back across the stage to snatch up the mic from Mr. Bauer. "Y'ALL HUSH UP, YA HEAR? WE'RE STARTIN!'" With a quick pivot, she turned to the principal.

Taking the mic from her, he nodded in appreciation.

"Thank you, kindly. Now, welcome to the Bellmont third Annual Talent Show. We've got some special acts from some very talented youngsters."

Phil peeked through the curtains from the side of the stage to gander at the audience. From what he could see, most of the student body was there. He was even able to spot June and Ben from the yearbook club. As he squinted, he caught sight of Lisa Cooper sitting towards the end of an aisle wearing a black turtle neck and of course, her over-sized heart pendant. Happy as he was that they came, he wasn't scanning for them. Then he spotted her.

Cara Miller was second row, center. Of course, being groped by Mr. Johnny Black. Just behind them were his Tweedle-dee and Tweedle-dumb, Tom Armstead and Billy Abbot. Cara fidgeted and rolled her eyes as Johnny dropped filthy nothings into her ear. At the sight of this, Phil adjusted his posture and pulled his shoulders back. It was now or never.

After finishing his spiel about hometown pride and audience behavior, Principal Bauer announced their first act. "First up, we have a Miss Kelly Samson to give us a taste of bluegrass." He stepped aside as the spotlight moved to a stout girl with long brown hair. Whipping her hair out of the way, she placed a fiddle to her shoulder and fastened it tight against her chin. After a long, striking chord, she broke into a rendition of the Appalachian classic, "Blue Moon of Kentucky." The audience clapped along, and Phil's mother fought the urge to break into a clog along-side the stage. Kelly finished to a rousing applause. Taking a bow, she walked offstage and passed Phil.

"Great job, Kelly!" he whispered. She smiled and nodded.

Principal Bauer appeared and reached into his coat to draw out an index card. "Next up, we have a Mr. Vincent Carter to work his magic."

A figure of a top hat and cape started towards the spotlight from the opposite end of the stage. Behind him was Mrs. Milton with a rolling table adorned with a black tablecloth. Removing his top hat, he grasped both sides to flip the hat's opening to the audience. After they observed it was empty, he placed the hat upside down on the black table. Of course, he pulled out the predictable chain of strung- together scarves. As much as Phil tried to enjoy the act, his nerves were getting the best of him. He began to bite his nails down to the bed.

Hearing the clicking, Gladys turned and swatted his hand from his face. "Relax now, ya hear?"

The run-of-the-mill, five-minute magic act over; it was Phil's turn. Time to take hold of his finest hour.

Vincent wheeled the table off stage as Mr. Bauer approached the light. "Thank you very much for that fine magic display, Vince." He squinted at his card before announcing, "Next up is Phillip Clemens who's gonna sing us a mighty fine song. Take it away, Mr. Clemens!"

Phil didn't move. His mother looked to him, "Well, go on, Phil! This is your moment!" She gave him a shove and he started across the stage.

The bright light encircling Mr. Bauer was almost blinding. Phil used his hand as a visor so he could see to grab the microphone. As he took it from the principal, he heard Johnny and his crew softly snickering. Practically drenched in sweat from the heat of the lights (and his own anxiety) Phil unsteadily raised the mic to his lips and the auditorium heard his heavy breaths.

The yearbook kids leaned forward in anticipation. Lisa peeked over her hand covering her face. She couldn't bear the sight of him embarrassing himself. Johnny and the boys smiled, awaiting a laughable performance.

Taking one last deep breath, Phil looked straight at Cara Miller. "Th-th-th-this one's for you, Miss Miller." A look of confusion dawned on her face, and Johnny sank his brows in anger.

Without room for pause, Phil belted out a cracked, "CAAARAAA MIIIAAAA WHYYYY...MUST WE SAAAAY G'BYYYYE?"

The audience erupted in laughter. Lisa hunched over with her face in her hands. June and Ben exchanged looks and Phil's mother pressed her fist to her mouth. Still, Phil went on with an outstretched arm to Cara, "Each time we part, my heart wants to DIIIIIIE!"

Tom stood up and chucked a wad of paper at Phil, hitting him square in the chest. Stunned, Phil stopped short, mid-lyric.

Cara stood up and whipped around. "STOP IT, TOMMY!"

Tom scoffed and pointed to Phil. "What? You in love with this retard err somethin?'"

"I SAID STOP IT!" Cara stomped her foot.

Johnny grabbed the end of her sweater and yanked her back into her seat. A hush fell over the audience, all eyes on a tearful Phil standing slump-shouldered in heartbreak and embarrassment. He dropped the microphone where he stood and rushed off the stage into his mother's arms. He wept for a moment until Gladys pushed him aside and began to march loudly across the stage in her white pumps. The look she wore scared Principle Bauer into staying right where he was.

She snatched up the mic and pointed a finger at the boys. "YOU!" She practically screamed it.

The entire assembly stared at her in awe as she gripped the mic tighter. "You boys will pay for the things you do in this life or the next—if I have to see to it MYSELF!"

"And YOU!" she pointed to Cara. "You need to stop runnin' with these no-good skirt chasers. Grow up, and appreciate the things like what my boy did here for you tonight!"

Gladys gave one last look of angry defiance before dropping the microphone. As deafening feedback sounded from the speakers, she marched back across the stage to grab her boy's hand. "C'mon, baby. This town ain't ready for real talent and real heart, anyhow!"

Phil kept on weeping as they made their exit from the building.

Meanwhile, a nervous Principal Bauer crept across the stage and picked up the microphone. "Uh...thank you, Mr. Clemens. Now, next up we have a..."

Despite his mother's rant about his being misunderstood by a buncha hypocritical assholes, Phil couldn't stop crying, from the time they left the school to when he pulled his bed sheets over his head. What was supposed to be the best night of his life turned into the worst. It took him a long time to get to sleep.

Phil awoke at eleven a.m., relieved it was the weekend. He didn't have to face the kids at school just yet. In his sleepy stupor, he made his way slowly through the living room and into the kitchen. There was a note left on the table with a five-dollar bill next to it. It read: *Dear Phil, Your Daddy is still sleeping. I took your granny to Wally's Fruit Mart. Here's some money to go to Jay's record store. Remember, you're a gift from God and you'll always be my shining star. Love, Momma*

A warm smile came over Phil's face, immediately followed by an excited grin and quiet shriek. So many new records he'd been wanting to hear. Darting from the kitchen, he licked his lips eagerly on the way back to his room to get changed. Of course, he was reaching with blind haste through his closet and pulling out the first things he'd found. Olive corduroys and white tee it was, for today.

The whole walk to town, he tried to relax and breathe in the air of a new day. Still, he found himself shaking flashbacks of last night's embarrassing events as he walked. He wouldn't be able to live down much of it. But he'd gotten his point across to Cara. At the very least, it was out there, how he felt about her. He could be satisfied with that.

Gravel and dirt became concrete and asphalt once he reached town a few miles down the road. The quaint little downtown of Florence was lined with Mom-and-Pop shops and parking meters. Phil's shoes shed pebbles and dirt as he scuffled down the sidewalk. The town was bustling from Appliance on the Avenue to Hunter's Candy Shop. Eager to get his hands on some vinyl, he picked up the pace after Riley Bros Diner. He could practically smell the album sleeves.

Fine Tune's doorbell chimed as he entered. Phil stopped to pan over the buffet of musical genres, rubbing his hands together. The orange and green beaded curtains parted and local DJ, Jukebox Jay, stepped out from behind the counter wearing a plaid button up and thick rimmed glasses.

Throwing his hands up, he shouted. "Phil, my boy!"

Phil wrapped his arms around Jay once the DJ made his way from behind the counter. "He-he-he-hey, Juke-b-b-box!"

Jay pulled away to slap Phil on the arm. "Hear you been charmin' some fine felines with some musical rhymes! Far out, man!"

Phil hung his head. Of course it'd be the talk of the town. How could he have been so foolish?

Jay pet his goatee and looked over his glasses at an embarrassed Phil. "Aw, c'mon now, kid! It took some sass and brass to do what you did, my friend! Remember, this is a town full of squares with gray hairs and lame-game cats, ya dig?"

Phil couldn't help but chuckle. "M-m-m-man! It's like I'm listening to the ra-ra-radio!"

Running his fingers through his salt and pepper crew-cut, Jay laughed heartily. "Well man, what can I say? I only breathe the air in waves. The airwaves, my man. And besides," Jay cocked his head, "I been the odd man out before. Hell, I was teased up and down the halls of Bellmont by jocks who couldn't get hip to the latest and greatest 'cause it came from the 'weirdo west.' But bein' the odd man out made me the far-out cat I am today!" He looked around his shop. "Now, I'm livin' the dream my friend and those jocks are still crop dustin' plowboys! Ya dig?"

Phil smiled and rubbed his hands on his pants. He stood for a moment staring at Jay as if he'd forgotten the purpose of his visit.

Jay broke the awkward silence, "Anyways, what can I do ya for, brother?"

Phil shook his head and snapped to. "Oh yeah! Momma gave me five dollars and I'm-l-l-lookin' to hear somethin' n-n-new!"

Jay swung an arm around Phil's shoulder. "Boss! I just got some fresh sounds outta movin' Motown!"

Shoulder to shoulder, they strolled past the record stands. "As a cat with his heart on his sleeve, you must not leave..." Jay plucked a record from the row, "without this."

Phil grasped the record at both ends and gazed at the cover. On it were four black gentlemen in a well-suited, stylized photograph. He was intrigued. "The F-f-four Tops?"

"That's right, my man! Bringin' you that hit-home heartache with 'The Same Old Song.'"

Jay hunted around for other Motown records while Phil was busy staring at the record and scanning through the track list.

Lurking around the entrance were a menacing Tom, Billy, and Johnny. They watched him move about the store. Johnny had never seemed so focused in his life as his angry eyes zeroed in on the unsuspecting Phil. He spit his chew between his short responses to the others. Nothing would make him happier than getting a message across to some clown who'd been trying to make a fool out of him.

"What are you supposin' we do, Johnny?" Billy asked, flustered.

Tom slapped the wool covering Billy's chest on his varsity jacket. "Stop askin' so many damned questions! Johnny's gonna tell us when he figures it out, OK?"

Without breaking focus, Johnny responded, "I think we're just gonna scare him a lil.' That's all. Remind him that he's nothin' but a sissy boy who needs to keep his idiot-mouth shut."

Enamored with Diana Ross's radiant smile and delicate frame, Phil decided to snag a Supremes record too.

Jay gave him a firm slap on the back before taking his place behind the register. "I'm excited for you to get into the Rhythm & Blues, my friend."

Phil placed the records on the counter before digging for his five-dollar bill, saying, "Well, I'mma gon' go straight home and p-p-p-put these on!"

Jay slid the slender vinyls into a thin paper sack and smiled in approval, handing them over. "Yeah, man! Be sure to let me know what you think of 'em!"

Tom, Billy, and Johnny had moved aside from the entrance so as not to be seen immediately. They wore rebel sneers with mobster demeanors while they waited. The bell chimed and Phil was startled when he met them face-to-face. So much so that he dropped his purchase. The boys let out a collective chuckle as Johnny snatched the bag from the ground.

Pulling the albums out, Johnny scoffed, "Pfft...Boy, what you doin' listenin' to this nigger music, anyhow?"

Phil looked caught off guard as Billy whistled a verse of Dixie Land. Angered, yet scared, Phil reached out his hand. "Th-th-those are mine, Johnny." He then sheepishly added, "And they ain't niggers."

Johnny held his hands up as if surrendering. "Whoa, whoa, now," he said. "No need to get hostile. Besides," Johnny leaned in close, "a friend wouldn't be serenadin' his friend's girl, would he?"

Phil swallowed hard as Johnny slapped the records into his chest. He began to sweat.

Backing away, Johnny laughed at Phil's panic. "Boy, I'm just jokin' with you! I'm sure it's aaalll a big misunderstandin,' right boys?"

Tom garbled through a wad of chew. "Yeah, a misunderstandin.'"

Phil smiled, relieved. "Gee f-fellas, thanks for takin' it s-s-s-so well!"

Johnny shrugged. "Course, good buddy." He slyly moved behind Phil and firmly dropped his hands upon his shoulders. Bending to Phil's ear, he whispered, "In fact, me and the boys were a thinkin' that you could join our crew...if'n you're up to the test."

"Really, Johnny?"

"Really, Phil. We really think you have what it takes to be one'a us."

Tom and Billy smiled villainously. Phil swiftly turned to Johnny. Looking wide-eyed as if he'd met a superhero, he asked, "W-what do I gotta do, Johnny?"

Johnny drew a toothpick before responding, "Just come with us and we'll show ya."

Phil smiled in child-like approval.

Johnny nodded towards a red pickup just in front of the record store. "Hop in the back with the boys and we'll get this shindig started."

With an arm around Phil, Johnny marched him to the bed of the truck. Tom and Billy followed suit. Phil carefully dropped his paper bag into the bed before climbing over. When he took his seat towards the cab, he found himself sandwiched by Tom and Billy. Phil reached for his vinyl and once again hugged the records close as he looked around. Before them were a tire iron, a bent tire rim, and some boating rope. Johnny started up the truck and headed down the main road out of town. The truck rocked from gravel while they made their way back to the country, passing miles of cornfields and unfamiliar roads.

Phil looked confused. "Wh-where are we?"

Tom and Billy smiled to each other.

"We're almost there, Phil," Tom responded. "Don'tchu worry none."

Finally, the truck slowed and pulled to the right, coming to a stop. Phil looked slightly alarmed and he hugged the paper sack even tighter.

Johnny exited the vehicle and slapped his hands together. "Alright! First test!"

Immediately, Tom and Billy sprang into action. Phil was stunned when Billy suddenly jerked the records from his arms. Tom pulled his legs from under him. Nearly bashing his head onto the floor of the truck, Phil let out a panicked yell. He kicked wildly as Tom and Billy restrained him. Johnny lowered the tail gate.

"Easy, now!" Tom shouted.

"Stop it!" Phil cried. "Wh-wh-what are you doin'?"

Johnny grabbed up the spool of rope. "This is the first test, ya hear? You're gon' be OK!"

Tom chuckled as Johnny got a tight grip on Phil's ankles. Pinning them down with his shins, Johnny unraveled the rope and began circling it around Phil's legs. Through the constant squirming and shouting, he tied a hefty sailor's knot at Phil's knees. Having completed his hog-tie, Johnny nodded to the boys. "Alright, let him out!"

Hauling Phil at the wrists, the boys jerked him upright as they stood. In a hurry, they danced him to the edge and threw him to the rocky Earth's floor with a loud thud. The dust and dirt that rose nearly blinded poor Phil. The boys laughed, seeing him try to catch the breath that was knocked clean from his lungs.

Phil squirmed like a turtle on its back and Johnny watched him for a few moments before he leaned forward, his hands on his knees. "You gotta take some nicks and scrapes if you wanna be hard like us, son!" He slammed the tail gate shut and jumped out to tie the rope's loose end to the hitch.

Phil's voice was strained, "Please...stop..."

"Boy, you gon' be just fine! I told you!" Johnny smirked and made his way around the truck.

Billy looked at Phil, concerned. "Now, we ain't gonna hurt him TOO bad like this, are we?"

Rolling his eyes and releasing a huff, Johnny spat back, "Look, we ain't goin' but a mile and I'm doin' fifteen. Ain't shit gon' happen but a few nicks. I just know what'll really scare this lil turd into ever thinkin' he can mess with me or my girl again." He opened the driver door.

Billy looked to the truck's bed floor and slowly nodded. It was clear he wasn't completely comfortable with the idea. He shot another look to Phil, whimpering fearfully on the ground.

Tom peered around Billy's shoulder and pointed a stern finger in his face. "Don't you be goin' soft on us now, boy!"

"I ain't! Now get yer fuckin' finger outta my face!"

"HEY! Shut up and let's get this show on the road while it's still light out!" With that, Johnny swung his body into the driver's seat and the boys clutched the sides of the truck where they sat. When the ignition started, Phil began to hyperventilate.

He was scared shitless.

Billy tried to smile along with Tom. Despite his conscience getting the best of him, his pride won. Being a team player was what it was always about, right? Johnny pressed a soft foot on the gas. It took a moment for the rope to straighten. Once the slack was taut, Phil's body was dragged across the rocky terrain. He screamed as his shirt raised and his back streaked with small lacerations from jagged pebbles. Tom threw his head back and laughed but Billy looked on in fear. Shooting a narrow-eye to the rear view, Johnny applied a little more pressure to the gas.

Billy and Tom shot each other a look when the truck sped up. At nearly twenty miles per hour, Phil's head bounced about like a rag doll, bloodying up his scalp. Seeing Phil's hair adorned with streaks of red plasma, Tom beat on the back window. "HEY, JOHNNY! SLOW DOWN! SLOW DOWN!"

With eyes locked on the road, Johnny was unreachable in his rage-induced trance. His pride hurt, his girl labeling him insensitive, him and his friends being made to look like dummies... These complaints came as flashes in time, hypnotic.

Instead of slowing the vehicle, he floored it.

The truck slung Phil's body from left to right over the road. He wailed for his life as the skin on his arms began to peel. The dirt burned his raw wounds like salt. His green pants became a shredded, blood spattered mess. Johnny didn't stop, though. The ground clawed at Phil's flesh, ripping his elbows and forearms to gleaming white bone.

Billy beat on the back window relentlessly. "JESUS CHRIST, STOP!"

Tom's eyes were frozen on Phil as shock set in. His disturbing wide-eyed silence spoke of a boy witnessing a murder. The earth took claim of all three layers of Phil's flesh. Tears streamed from the boys' faces as they watched his head bounce even higher.

Billy was begging for Phil's life at this point. "STOP! STOP! STOOOOOOOP!"

Shaking the spell, Johnny slammed on the brakes.

The boys slid, crashing hard into the tail gate. Phil's body slipped under the truck. When the dust settled, Billy and Tom caught a glimpse of a heavy breathing Johnny slumped over his steering wheel. The boys looked to each other in a panic before hopping out of the truck. They crouched to look underneath the second they hit the ground.

What they saw was merely a lumpy shadow.

Billy gulped hard before calling to Phil with a shaken voice, "...Phil?"

No response.

"Jesus Christ..." Billy whispered through his tears. "We killed him."

Tom grabbed the rope at the hitch. "No we didn't...No we didn't!"

Three tugs was all it took to reveal Phil's body of maroon pulp. Tom turned to vomit at the sight of the cracked skull. He could see clear to the brain. As Tom was expelling, Billy slowly rose to meet Johnny's panicked face.

"I-I—" Johnny nervously began. He was sweating like a man facing the gallows.

Billy bit the lower lip of his sweat and tear-sopped face. Without hesitation, he reached back and threw a right hook. Johnny fell to the ground, covering his blood-spattered nose with his hands.

"Fuck you, Johnny!" Billy cried. "Now we're all fucked!"

Johnny sat silent in pain. He fully accepted Billy's response. He knew the words were true.

Tom wiped the mucous from his mouth. He breathed heavily and he struggled to stand upright. "This isn't happening..." he whispered to himself. "It's not happening, man..." Slowly, looking back to Phil's body, Tom sniffled. He immediately swung back to his original position to throw up again.

Billy closed his eyes and turned his chin to the sky. There were no words left. They were involved in the murder of Phil Clemens. Black and white. Plain and simple.

Johnny leaned his hands back to push himself from the ground. When he rose, he smeared blood from his nose onto his leather sleeve. Tom opened his eyes to the sky. He still couldn't pull it together to look at Johnny.

Nodding in acknowledgement of the recent events, Johnny spoke, "Well...what now?"

Tom composed himself enough to turn and face Johnny. "What do you mean? We're goin' to fry, asshole!"

Johnny pursed his lips tight in efforts to keep from crying. "No. No we ain't." He then looked to Billy who finally met his eyes. He said slowly, pausing between each word, "Cause we ain't sayin' shit."

The boys gave Johnny a hard stare.

"Well?" Johnny raised his arms to their surroundings. "Who the hell was here? The CORN?"

With that, he drew a switchblade from his jean pocket and went to work on cutting the rope from the hitch. The boys exchanged looks. Their eyes were glazed over with a thick layer of terror. When the rope snapped in two, it fell to the ground. Johnny whipped off the piece still hanging from the hitch. He wielded the knife at the boys. Threatened, they backed away. Tightening his grip on the blade, Johnny instructed them in a maddened voice, "Now, get in the truck."

With their eyes still on Johnny, they moved slowly to follow orders. Johnny exhaled deep before he gave one last look to the late Phil Clemens, closed the switchblade, and made his way into the driver's seat. They sped away, and Billy watched Phil's carcass shrink in the distance.

It was in God's hands now.

* * * * *

Gladys burst through the door of Jay's Fine Tunes. She was frantic to find her son who'd been gone for hours now. Jay flew through the beaded curtains to witness a mother in a state of panic.

"Jay! My boy come through here?"

"Yeah, Mrs. C! He was in here. But he left about a few hours ago. He didn't come home?"

Gladys shook her head and began to cry. A policeman came in from behind her and braced her shoulders. Jay ran to her also. "Don't cry, Mrs. C! I'll help you find him!"

The police officer gently pulled her from the entrance. Jay switched the open sign around and reached for his keys. Locking the building, he nodded to them. Once they had all piled into the large Chrysler, Officer Lee switched on the siren.

They made their way swiftly using the gravel road that led out of downtown. A silent thirty minutes went by driving on the rocky, country roads. Gladys clutched her crucifix charm and muttered under her breath.

Officer Lee looked to the rear view at Jay. "When was he in your store?"

"I dunno, man...like, three hours ago. He just bought some records and left, like normal."

In another few minutes, Officer Lee narrowed his eyes in front of him. Noting his sudden focus, Gladys leaned forward to see a lumpy figure lying in the middle of the road. As they came closer, it was clear the figure was human.

Gladys shook her head and choked back tears. "No...no...it ain't." Then she screamed, "That ain't my boy!"

Officer Lee slowed and stopped the vehicle ten feet in front of the body. Jay's mouth dropped in disbelief and he clutched onto his hair. Slowly, the three of them exited the car. Officer Lee sped ahead of Gladys to get a full view of the scene. He peered over the swarm of flies surrounding the sack of gore. Gladys put her hands to her mouth as she scurried behind in her white heels. One look was all it took. She knew it was her son.

"NOOOOOOO! GOD DAMNIT!" She hit ground and crawled on her bare knees through the gravel. Small stones embedded into her shins and one of her shoes slipped off. Falling over her only son's blood-soaked body, she whimpered through a mess of tears, "Not my baby...not my baby." Her yellow sundress soaked up the blood that oozed from what was left of her boy. Jay fell to his knees behind her, desperately trying to pull her from Phil.

Officer Lee walked back to his squad car, leaned in through the open window, and pulled the CB mic to his mouth. "We found the Clemens boy. Over."

An officer responded inquiring of his whereabouts.

"We got his body here on Tallahatchie road near the cornfields. Looks like there's been an...accident. ...Over."

* * * * *

Johnny's mind was racing a mile a minute to justify

150

his horrific deed. Sure, his judgment was impaired by blind rage. But the Black name carried in this town. He sure as hell wouldn't want to disappoint Daddy. Standing by while some retard with a crush made a fool out of him and his friends? No, sir.

Tom and Billy kept a fearful stare on a seemingly possessed Johnny, the truck rocking as they made their getaway through the bumpy countryside.

Feeling their burning glare, Johnny whipped an unnerving look their way. "What? Y'all should be thankin' me!"

With faces that melted from anxiety to shock, Tom and Billy looked at each other.

"What in the fuck for?" Tom shouted.

Johnny bit his lip and shook his head. He spit as he spoke, "That lil retard was a skid anyways! He was playin' with my girl in front of the whole school!"

His friends' eyes widened at the audacity of his words, the insanity of what he was trying to say.

"I don't take kindly to that shit 'n neither should you!"

Billy readjusted his posture as he fixed on the distance. "Take us home, Johnny."

Meanwhile, it was taking the broad build of Officer Lee and the 6'5" former defensive lineman, Sheriff Edwards, to restrain Judson, who screamed, "I'MMA KILL THEM SONSA BITCHES!"

They looked to Gladys to talk some sense into her husband while they wrestled him on the living room floor. However, she wore a cold stare at the window, chain smoking in shock and mourning. It's not as if she would have stopped him, anyway.

"Judson, I swear on the life of my son, I promise you we're gonna find who did this!" The Sheriff was desperate. He didn't want to resort to more drastic measures.

With his face smashed to the carpet, Judson replied, "I...I know who did this..."

The Sherriff dug in harder. "You ain't got no proof it was anybody! Now we're gon' investigate this here matter and justice will be served! I can promise you that!"

A few silent moments went by without a fight from Judson. Slowly, the two officers backed away. They stood and watched the sweaty and enraged mammoth-of-a-man begin to sob where he lay, then gave a nod to each other before heading towards the front door.

Mrs. Clemens remained in her chair, puffing away. They paused to get her attention but failed to move her.

"We'll call you when we get some leads, Mrs. Clemens. I'm truly sorry for your loss." Officer Lee tipped his hat with the words.

Paying no mind to either of them, she took another drag as they walked out the door.

Across town, Johnny was experiencing his own loss of words. Having dropped his accomplices off, he was dreading something just as much as his legal fate: his father.

Mr. Black rocked between the porch pillars of his plantation, dancing a willow branch between his fingers while he awaited his tardy son. Johnny pulled in the drive and turned off the ignition. He released a hefty sigh when he saw his father's tall silhouette there on the porch, stepping down to greet him.

"Boy, where the hell you been?"

Johnny put his hands in his pockets and looked at the ground. "Oh, well there was a problem with Billy's dad's truck and um...he needed an extra hand. I done bumped my nose slidin' underneath, heh."

Buford brought his fist to his hip. "Sounds like Billy's dad's problem, don't it?"

Johnny closed his eyes and sighed. He knew there

was no way around this one.

Mr. Black's eyes focused in on the bed of the truck, curious. Watching his father take a step forward to look more closely Johnny shut his eyes in anguish.

He'd forgotten about Phil's records.

His father pulled the records from the thin paper sack and took in the cover images. "Boy...you mean to tell me you were late cause you were out buyin' NIGGER MUSIC?"

"Paw, I..." Before he could continue, Johnny felt the burn of several tiny lacerations from his father's sharp switch. He crouched as his father wailed on him in their driveway. After almost fifteen strikes, his father stopped beating him to break the records over his knee. Pieces of colorful cardboard and black vinyl laid at his feet.

"Pick this shit up!"

Tears welled in Johnny's eyes as his father marched back inside.

Leaving his humiliated son in the driveway, Buford threw the switch across the living room. It happened to strike the television just as reports of the Phillip Clemens Tragedy were coming through. The words "A student of Bellmont High..." caught his attention. He stared at the screen intensely from behind their pearl chaise lounge.

Images of blood-stained gravel flashed intermittently as a tall, suited man spoke into the camera. "As you can see, we're standing here on Tallahatchie road, a few miles outside of downtown Florence. The late Phillip Clemens was found just a few hours ago with what appear to be wounds as a result of severe road rash. With respect to you folks watching at home, we won't go into further detail. However, the coroner has stated that it appears his cause of death was a result of brain hemorrhaging. Officials say foul play has not been established but is a hard speculation at this point. More on this story as it develops."

Buford leaned forward, scooped up the remote, and turned off the set. He stared hard at the blank screen for a few moments, then looked to the floor and pondered what he'd just seen. Hearing some scuffling gravel, he turned to see his son dusting his pants off in the drive. He shook the disturbance quickly with a pivot and headed to his study.

That same evening Lisa settled in with a joint in her folks' shed, ready for Jukebox Jay's nightly show. Her eyes widened mid-drag upon hearing Jay's shaken voice.

"Today," he choked, "today...um...we lost a really cool kid and one of my pals, Phil Clemens. I um..." he paused to sniffle. "Pfft, I can't even believe I'm sayin' this, man... He was found dead on Tallahatchie road this afternoon."

Lisa flicked her joint in the corner and sprang to her feet. Grasping the stereo at both ends, she shook her head in disbelief.

"We don't know exactly what happened..." The radio was silent as he stopped to collect his thoughts for a moment. Then he went on, "But I can still remember when his mom brought him into the store for the first time. It was the kid's seventh birthday and he couldn't stop singin' 'That'll be the Day.' And so..."

Jay let the breakdown happen, sobbing, "I sold him his first record!"

Lisa clenched her shirt over her heart as her own tears began to stream.

"Why, man?" He asked himself aloud. "Who would do this?"

Lisa turned slowly from the radio and sank along the splintered wall. That was a good question. She wandered deep into her own dark thoughts as Jay finished, "Sorry... Anyway, this one's for you, Phil. Say 'hey' to Buddy for me."

As the rockabilly vocal styling of the late Mr. Holly

echoed off the shed's walls, Lisa retrieved the joint for one last toke. Her look of sorrow turned into a scowl as the high set in. "I gotta get the hell outta here," she whispered to the wall. She licked her index finger, snubbed the hots out, and placed the Mary Jane from whence it came, tucked behind a snow shovel. Slowly, she rose to her feet, exited the shed, and made her way back to the house.

Lisa was determined to make her voice heard. She stomped up the porch steps, swung open the door, and let it slam behind her. She now had the attention of her quaint, crocheting mother and pipe-smoking father. "I NEED TO GO BACK TO CALI."

Her mother sighed, dropping her needles into her lap. Withdrawing the pipe from his mouth, her father spoke sternly from his easy chair. "Lisa, for the last time, your mother and I came here to take care of Granny when she was sick—"

"GRANNY'S DEAD NOW!"

He put up his hands to cease her yelling. "I know that, Lisa. But we have to think about this family's values. California's slums are on the rise and I can't tell you how much I hated you hanging out with those Beatniks. They're nowhere people, Lisa. Nowhere."

Lisa clenched her fists. "NOWHERE? I'll tell you what nowhere is! This nowhere hillbilly shit hole and its wacked-out mindset!"

Her mother jumped to her feet. "LISA!"

"NO!" Lisa interrupted. "My friends and I were trying to get the West and this rest of this country to go somewhere and to take off the blinders!"

"Oh, here we go..." Her father rolled his eyes.

"This-this-this tripped out realm of cookie-cutter society morals in a pit of stagnation...!"

Her father stood up. "ALRIGHT! I've had enough!" We're not going back to California and that's final!"

Lisa's left middle finger was mid-extension when there was a gentle rap at the door. It startled Lisa out of the moment.

"Who could that be at this hour?" her father asked, taking cautious steps towards the door. He looked through the keyhole, frowned, and opened the door. "Can I help you, young lady?"

There was a young girl looking sheepish as she stood on the porch in her letter jacket. She took a nervous breath. "Um..." she started. "I'm looking for Lisa."

He smiled and turned and looked at Lisa, who was still heaving a bit. "Your friend is here."

Struck with confusion, Lisa went to the door. She was a bit startled to see Cara not only in her presence, but on her front porch. Scooting past her father, she stepped onto the porch. In closing the door, she heard her mother inquire, "Lisa has friends?"

Two opposite ends of the spectrum stared silently at each other for a moment. Lisa was the one to break before an intimidated Cara. "Uh, hey." Lisa would never admit to herself that they, in fact, intimidated each other.

"Hi," Cara began. "I wanted to tell you I'm sorry about your friend, Phil. He was a really nice kid and uh..."

Lisa interrupted. "How did you know where I live?"

Cara laughed a bit. "We ride the same bus. You get dropped off just before I do."

"Why did you come here to tell me this?"

Cara's pride felt a blow. "Well, I just thought I'd offer my condolences. Sorry, I ain't no hard ass like you."

"You wish you were, though."

"Go to hell."

Cara was stomping down the porch stairs when Lisa replied, "I'm already there."

Cara froze. In that moment, she realized if there was

only one thing the two of them shared, it was despair. She turned and faced Lisa with weepy eyes. "You don't know me. You think you do. But you really don't."

Lisa put her hands to her hips and gazed upon a surprisingly vulnerable Cara. It was then Lisa stepped outside herself and surrendered the cynicism. "I may not speak to you, but I see you."

Cara broke down at these words. Weeping, she gripped her hair by the handful. "I may as well have killed him!"

Lisa trotted down the steps. "What? Why did you just say that?"

Cara dropped her arms to her side and looked to the ground "I don't know... I don't even know what I'm saying."

Lisa put her hand on Cara's shoulder "Look at me. Do you know something?"

"No. I don't know a damn thing. I just know that I could have done more. I shouldn't be with Johnny. I shouldn't have let them make fun of him and now he's gone and that was one of the last goddamn moments of his life—" Her voice raised as she sobbed, "He'll never get his life back AND IT'S ALL MY FAULT!"

Lisa tried to bring Cara down a notch. She wanted to provide some comfort but still keep a barrier between them. "It wasn't your fault. Maybe you shouldn't be with Johnny but what's that got to do with anything? It's your fault for not having any self-respect, maybe. But Phil's death was nothing you did, I'm sure of it."

Cara nodded, taking deep breaths to get herself under control. She smiled and looked at Lisa. "Do me a favor, Lisa. Don't tell anyone I was here, OK?"

Lisa dropped her hand from Cara's shoulder and laughed. She started back up the steps. "No problem. I don't want anyone knowing I was talking to your nutty self."

* * * * *

Later that night Tom Armstead tossed and turned in a pool of his sweat. The scenes seemed to play on a loop, a gallery of Phil's final moments. His ears rang with a chorus of Phil's cries and he couldn't stop thinking of the steam that rose from the kid's torn skin. It was either the memory of heat rising from Phil's oozing flesh or the smell of death and burnt rubber staining his nostrils that prompted him to vomit once more.

The cool Kentucky breeze blew his white drapes and made them dance like ghosts, startling Tom every time they moved. Eventually he shot up from his bed, grabbed the French windows, and pulled them shut. The drapes ceased their cryptic waltz, and Tom released the window knobs. He dropped his arms and sighed in mental exhaustion.

His undershirt was soaked with perspiration. Walking back towards his bed, Tom began to pull his white tee over his head when he felt the breeze again.

Just as his shirt passed his head, his neck jolted from a violent shove. His exposed face was met with an indescribable burn and teeth-clenching pain, and his ears were flooded with ringing as if a bomb had gone off. Warm blood rained from his skull and he watched it puddle on the floor before blindness set in. The young Mr. Armstead lost all cognitive ability to speak or reason; he began to tremor violently. A shadowy figure stepped through the window, put its foot to Tom's chest, reached down and dislodged the meat cleaver from his skull.

The figure stood back to survey the scene for a few moments. There lay Mr. Tom Armstead in a pool of blood big enough to fill a small creek. His arms and legs were sprawled and his tongue had fallen out of his mouth. The figure shook excess brain matter from the knife. It splattered onto Tom's split open face. With that, the killer's shadowy image crawled stealthily back through the window and out of sight.

Come Monday morning, Bellmont High was buzzing like a kicked hornets' nest. Johnny Black walked slowly through the halls, whispers of a town serial killer falling on his ears. When he reached his locker, he peeled off his varsity jacket and threw it over his arm. Just as he began to turn the lock, he jumped at the sight of Billy Abbot standing at his side. They locked eyes before Billy said, "Tommy's dead."

Johnny narrowed his eyes in confusion and stammered.

Billy's fist gave a good pound to his locker and Johnny jumped back. "Did you hear what I said, Johnny? Tom was found in his room last night. Someone done took a beef cleaver to his forehead."

Johnny shook his head in shock and disbelief. It just couldn't be true.

Billy leaned closer. "Someone knows, Johnny. Someone knows...and I don't want to be seen with you anymore. Stay away from me." With that, Billy pushed himself off the locker and stalked away.

A panicked Johnny took short breaths as he watched his former cohort march down the hall. He'd been worried about getting caught; it hadn't occurred to him to worry about being killed. The homeroom bell sounded while Johnny ran for the nearest bathroom, nausea overtaking him.

In room 202, Lisa sat next to an empty chair, tears rolling from her eyes as Mr. Keefe took attendance in a room of mortuary silence. Lisa bowed her onyx bob and silently mourned an innocent boy. A boy she called friend. A boy she called her only friend.

After the last name was read, Mr. Keefe hung his

head and took off his glasses. He pinched the bridge of his nose, struggling to find words. "Now...Y'all know what happened by now, so I ain't gonna get into details." He raised his head to address his classroom. "I don't know exactly what's goin' on and neither do y'all, but I don't wanna hear none of y'all speculatin' and spreadin' rumors. Phil and Tom were good boys and their family don't need any more stress than they've already got. Ya hear?" The room remained silent and Mr. Keefe donned his glasses once more. "Now students, please remember to have your emergency contacts updated with the office..." His voice trailed into nothingness to a Lisa who was miles away.

Later that afternoon, Gladys and Judson stood in their Sunday's best among the tombstones of Florence's First Methodist Cemetery. The fall sun shined down on Phil's casket as the Clemens watched their child being lowered into the Earth. An inconsolable Gladys clenched her husband's lapels in her black dress suit and satin pillbox hat. He held her tight and he too began to weep.

Pastor Winston was there to see over the ceremony. At the Clemens' request, only a small group was present, mostly family. Aside from muffled sobs and birds chirping, it was quiet. Even Pastor Winston, who always had a verse of enlightenment, found no words to fit this savagery. Dirt sounded against the oak coffin and Judson decided it was time to take his wife home. There was nothing left to be seen or said.

Gladys had the sudden desire to make dinner when Judson pulled their salmon station wagon in the drive. She wasn't hungry, and the kitchen was filled to the brim with baked goods and sympathy casseroles, but she wanted to make an effort towards feeling normal. Roast was Judson's favorite. Perhaps she could get him to eat.

Entering the front screen door, Gladys slid off her heels and made her way to the refrigerator. Judson solemnly took his place in his armchair as she threw a frozen roast into the sink. With plans to split the half frozen beef into chunks, she withdrew her trusty meat cleaver from its wooden block and set it on the counter.

She was reaching for a cutting board when she caught a glimpse of Sherriff Edward's car pulling up. In a fit of anger, she grabbed the still-frozen meat, unwrapped it, and plopped it onto the cutting board. She then picked up the cleaver and began to hack at the frozen bovine.

Judson slowly waddled to answer their knock at the front door. Officer Lee and Sherriff Edwards respectfully removed their hats once he opened it.

Feeling the weight of Judson's stare, Edwards raised his head to speak, "Mr. Clemens, I know the funeral was today and y'all been through a lot. I was just wonderin' if I could ask y'all a few questions at this time."

Judson looked to the ground then turned around to his wife. The strikes at the meat were loud enough to catch the attention of the officers on the front porch. They peered over Judson's shoulder to see her wielding the cleaver. Judson asked if she felt like answering their questions.

With her forehead glazed with sweat, she ceased hacking to simply say, "Not right now."

Judson shrugged and turned back to the shaken law enforcement. "Not right now," he repeated. "Come back tomorra maybe. We need a lil time."

The men nodded before putting their hats back on. They both started down the steps, hearing the door close behind them. Officer Lee stopped at the bottom of the stairs as Edwards walked past, looking at the ground and aligning the last image of Gladys in his mind with the events being investigated.

Studying him for a moment, Edwards simply said, "I know."

* * * * *

Cara was struggling to keep focus during cheer practice. The other girls took notice of her distracted behavior. Her head kept panning from the football field to the parking lot just outside the gates. Normally, she'd see the red pickup. Perhaps it was in a different spot today, but she doubted it.

Coach Leah raised her hand to signal a stop to the routine. "CARA!"

"I'm sorry, Coach."

Coach Leah crossed her arms over her clipboard. "Ya with us, honey?"

"Yeah, coach. Sorry 'bout that." Cara pulled her pony tail tight to show she was really with it.

But just as the cheer team prepared to complete one last run of the routine, the boys began to take the field for their practice. Cara held out hope that she would see Johnny. She didn't.

She did see Billy, however. With his chin to his practice jersey, he made his way to the fifty-yard line. To her coach's further dismay, Cara booked it towards Billy to find out just where her boyfriend was. Giving up, Coach Leah waved the girls off the field in a fit of frustration.

Slowing to a jog, Cara caught Billy's attention. His first instinct was to turn from her, though. She symbolized everything he wanted nothing to do with anymore.

"Billy!" she shouted. "Where's Johnny?"

Without looking at her, he mumbled, "I don't know."

He bent down to stretch his quads when she stood over him. "What do you mean you don't know? I ain't seen him all day..."

"I SAID I don't KNOW!"

Cara backed away then and darted across the field to

scoop up her backpack. Her first order of business was to call Johnny when she got home.

Back at the Black Estate, suspect interrogation was underway.

"Now, son," Officer Lee began. "We're just tryin' to find out where ever'body was Saturday 'round noon."

Johnny sat on the porch rocker, his leg shaking nervously. He nearly pissed himself from the pressure of Lee and Edwards' stares.

His father stood behind him with arms folded, wondering two things: Why the hell were they questioning his boy...and why the hell was his boy being antsy?

Finally, Johnny looked up and shrugged. "Pfft, I mean...I was with my friends downtown. Then I was helpin' one'a my friends with his dad's truck. That's it."

Sherriff Edwards withdrew a note pad and clicked his pen. "Can you give me their names, son?"

Johnny picked a bit at his nails before answering, "Yeah. Billy Abbot and Tommy Armstead."

The officers looked to each other, looked at Johnny's father, then back to a nervous Johnny.

"I'm truly sorry 'bout your friend, son," Edwards said. "You think these incidences are in any way connected?"

Johnny shook his head, looking out over the lawn. "Well, I mean I really don't know 'bout that. How could I? Isn't it your job to find out?"

Lee, who was slightly alarmed at his tone, said, "That last part was a little defensive, son."

Offended, Johnny's father stepped towards the officers just as Johnny shot up to say, "LOOK! I don't know nothin' bout anything that happened! I lost my friend and I barely knew Phil!"

"Alright, alright, son," Edwards said, trying to bring down the hostility. "We're just tryin' to collect all the information we can. Now we're askin' everybody. Not just you."

Johnny rubbed the back of his neck, a little embarrassed. "Sorry, I just want justice to prevail, sir." He put his hands in his pockets and continued, "I miss my friend and I'm sorry 'bout what happened to Phil."

"We are too, son," Edwards slid his notepad into his back pocket. "Well, I think we've got enough for now. We'll let you folks know if we need anythin' else."

Mr. Black nodded. "Thank you, officers. Y'all have a good day now."

Edwards and Lee tipped their hats and headed down the stairs to their squad car.

As they pulled away and drove off down the street, Johnny's father turned to look at his son. He stared hard for a moment before Johnny asked, "What?"

His father readjusted his posture. "Boy, you ain't got nothin' to do with none'a this, do ya?"

"Nothin' at all, Paw."

Mr. Black narrowed his eyes to simply say, "Good."

Inside the house, the phone rang and Johnny's mother answered. She called for Johnny and he flew into the house, glad to escape his father's gaze.

"Hello?...Yeah, look I wasn't feelin' good today...Uh huh... Yeah, I went home early... I dunno... some bug goin' around—LOOK, I really can't talk right now, alright, Cara? I ain't feelin' good and I'll see ya tomorra, anyhow!" He sighed into the receiver. "I know, but everything's OK, alright? I'll talk to ya tomorra... Alright, bye."

He gave another hefty exhale as he hung up the phone. A good night's rest would surely ease at least some of the pressure of this nightmare.

*   *   *   *   *

Billy was stuffing his jersey into his backpack before bed. *Johnny better show up tomorrow.* He didn't want anything to do with the guy, but he couldn't deal with Cara hounding him again. He'd give anything to go back to feeling normal. Probably wouldn't have that feeling anytime soon. Probably never again. He had to try, though.

The clock seemed to glare at him each time he rolled over in bed. Ten o'clock, eleven o'clock. Midnight. *This is fuckin' hopeless,* he thought to himself, rolling out of bed to head towards the bathroom. He reached the hall when he heard a floorboard sound from the living room. He was sure it wasn't his own. Curious, he tip-toed into the dark living area to be greeted with a harsh chill.

He rubbed his arms. "Jesus, it's freezing in here!" The porch light shined through an open window that faced the front porch. "Dammit, Daddy..." he muttered to himself.

He marched towards the window with intent to shut it when his entire body froze mid-step. His eyes crossed to focus in on a flesh-colored blur just at his nose. His bones rattled and he urinated on himself. The pain was the worst and most intense ten seconds he'd ever felt in his life or would ever feel again. Not even the blanket of warm blood that soaked his entire body could void the chill of death that engulfed him slowly.

Having taken a swipe sideways, the killer had planted the cleaver through the bridge of his nose. It was lodged pretty good and damn near went through the back of his skull, almost splitting his head into two halves. Before Billy could fall to his knees, the killer took a few good tugs to get the sideways implanted weapon from his face. The figure was thrown back when the cleaver finally gave way. With that, the empty shell of Billy Abbot staggered in mid-air. A wave of blood crashed at the killer's feet as Billy fell to the hard oak floors.

Tuesday morning was a dark dawn for the town of Florence. Nearly the entire police force was dispatched to ride around the streets and announce over their loud speakers, "School is closed throughout Boone County. Please do not send your children to school. All busses have been cancelled. We will keep you posted as to when it will resume. I REPEAT! SCHOOL IS CLOSED!"

While families were busy exchanging confused glances, Billy's father Dale Abbot was in a sweat, hastily loading a .338 Winchester Magnum. His hands shook, nearly dropping the bullets as he loaded. Lee and Edwards were imploring him to come out of his office where he'd barricaded himself.

"Mr. Abbot, come on out now," Edwards spoke to the door. "I know you're in a state of shock but we're doin' everything we can to catch this killer."

After a minute of silence, the officers nodded to each other, drew their pistols, and put their boots to the door. The wooden door split from its frame and the officers bounded into the room, taking aim at Mr. Abbot. He spun around in his office chair, dumbstruck, and his hand met with the butt of Lee's pistol. Upon the blunt strike, he dropped the rifle and Edwards stepped in to restrain him.

"Easy now, Dale!" Edwards yelled, grasping his flailing wrists.

"THAT WAS MY BOY! YOU UNDERSTAND?" Dale screamed as he burst into tears of rage, "MY SON!"

Dale was difficult to restrain because the chair twisted from left to right with all of his thrashing. Instinct and panic prompted Edwards to hit him on the back of the head with his gun. Dale slumped in his chair, unconscious while Lee looked at the sheriff in shock.

"We was outta options," Edwards shrugged. "Go back to the car and call another ambulance back here and make it quick."

Lee nodded then darted from the room.

* * * * *

Johnny's parents didn't try to stop him when he ran out the front door and into his truck, squealing away down the street. The news of Billy's grisly death was too much for him to bear.

He headed straight for Cara's. He knew she'd be both confused and devastated. It might also feel good to tell someone the truth. Besides, the poor girl deserved it. Whether she could handle it was another story. Pulling into the drive of her family's farmhouse, he saw her sitting on her porch step, sobbing. Her mother was beside her with her arms wrapped around her. She rocked her daughter back and forth in her maternal way.

Cara burst from her mother's embrace when she saw Johnny's truck pull in the drive. She ran to him as he stepped out of the driver's seat and pushed his shoulders back to look at his face.

Johnny hung his head for a moment, then raised it to look up at her and say, "Let's head into the barn. I gotta tell ya somethin.'" He threw an arm around her as they walked.

* * * * *

Gladys drew a heavy sigh as she parked, her driveway occupied by a police car yet again. Of course, there stood Lee and Edwards with her husband on the front porch. They all stared as they awaited her to exit the vehicle. Once she slammed the door, she jumped. The officers were speedily heading her way.

The gleam of Lee's handcuffs set her into a panic. "What do you think you're doin'?"

Edwards flashed the warrant. "Mrs. Clemens, we have a warrant for your arrest as a suspect in the murders of Thomas Armstead and William Abbot."

Lee grabbed her by the wrist and swung her around. He slapped the handcuffs on so fast, she barely had time to shout.

"What in the hell are you talkin' about? I didn't kill nobody! NOBODY!"

Judson pleaded from behind the officers, "I'm tellin' ya! She didn't do nothin'! Please, listen!"

Edwards turned around to face him as Officer Lee hauled Gladys off, kicking and screaming. "If she's innocent, she'll have no problem provin' that now, will she?"

Judson stared dumbly, not sure how to cope with what was happening. He yelled to his wife as she ducked into the police car, "Don't worry, baby! I'mma getcha outta this!"

* * * * *

Back at the Miller barn, Johnny's voice cracked as he confessed to Cara. She breathed through her hands, covering her mouth and soaking in his words. When he'd finished, Johnny bit his lip and waited for a response from a frozen Cara.

But her freezing was simply a brief, theatrical tableaux. An act before her face became as hard as granite.

She spoke to the dirt floor, "I knew that, Johnny."

Blood left his face and he was gray. "What?"

Her head low, Cara raised her eyes and repeated herself slowly, "I...knew...that." Then she began to laugh.

She stood and spun around, running to the barn door laughing the whole twenty feet. The door whined shut from her touch, and Johnny shook with terror.

"Cara?"

Upon the hard slam of the wooden lock, she hummed a bar from "This Magic Moment."

"What's happening, Cara?"

"I'm finally gettin' out of this town, Johnny." She leaned against the door. "I'm taking my self-respect with me... and you're coming, too."

Johnny wanted to run but his heels felt chained to the floor. His wide eyes watched her walking into the darkness at the far end of the barn, then he turned slowly and crept to the barn door. Before he made his exit, he called back to the shadows, "How did you know?"

At first, silence. No response. He gripped his hands around the barn lock, hoping to silently lift it and escape this unnerving situation.

He dropped it when he heard her voice.

"I had a feeling...but I wanted to believe it was you anyhow. So I could escape."

"Escape what?"

"A lifetime with you."

Cara ran out of the dark with a large cleaver above her head. Johnny instinctively ducked against the barn door, but this only set her up to strike him more easily. The first strike was to his left shoulder. He let out a howl.

As she repetitively chucked at his neck, Cara screamed at him, "Mommy! Hates! Me! She! Loved! You! I! Was! Never! Leaving! This! God! Damn! TOOOOOOWN!"

The severely damaged nerves in his neck, in some final act of desperation, sent misguided messages down his arms and to his finger, creating marionette strings for his right hand. Laying there, braindead, he jerked and twitched. Cara dropped the cleaver.

"I'm leaving now, Johnny," she whispered. "I'll see you later."

She heaved up the wooden block and stepped over what was left of Johnny. There was no going back.

Quietly, she opened the screen door and peeked into the house, scoping for any sight of her mother. There she was. Through the kitchen, Cara spotted the back of her head sitting in the wicker rocker on the front porch. The squeak of the chair would be the perfect silencer to her footsteps while she made her way through the house and to her father's office. It was time to pack.

A path of bloody footprints on the carpet was all Cara planned to leave behind. Entering the office, she looked to the right of a large moose' head. The sunlight from the high window danced on the long, black steel of the twelve gauge. She lifted it from its display and opened the desk drawer. Slamming a handful of shells onto the desk, she opened the chamber and packed in a live round.

The unmistakable racking sound caught her mother's ear. She turned and called through the front window, "Cara?"

That day, Cara finally left town.

That day, Cara finally had more listeners than just God and the walls.

That day, Cara left this life for good.

AFTERWORD
By Leah Lederman

The "Junk Lady" scene in the much-adored *Labyrinth* is one of the most terrifying moments I've ever witnessed in a movie. "It was all just a dream," Sarah says, hugging her teddy bear Lancelot, surrounded by all of her belongings... and then she opens the door.

It was a dream within a nightmare; taking the sweetness of the return home and turning it into revolting pulp—much like the worm in the apple she discovered moments before her encounter with the Junk Lady.

This terror, this gut-wrenching betrayal by the very objects and people we hold most dear, is what makes peace unattainable. We might find momentary solace, here or there, but the walls are always set to crumble. This... is madness.

Kasey Pierce's collection exemplifies, in remarkably colorful and chilling variations, this quest for normalcy: It's the rite of passage of an imaginary friend in "Luke;" leaving behind a hard life and starting fresh in "Bestia;" the preservation of the status quo, or what might have been, in "His Majesty." It's turning the same corner at

"Steiner and Holmes," again and again, only to find yourself in darkness or, worse yet, in Hell.

Each story in this collection, in some sense or another, features the walls caving in. There is no safe place. There is no going home. Each tale is either a hopeless descent to damnation or a hopeless ascent from damnation. There is no going home.

The truth is, I'm a bit of a scaredy-cat, though I'm not new to editing horror stories. When I edited Kasey's collection, though, it stuck with me. (I was eight months pregnant when I delved into "Luke," and it shook me to my bulbous pregnant core.) I thought about the stories late at night when I took the dog out, standing alone in my driveway, and I wasn't sure whether or not to look over my shoulder. If something was there, did I want to see it?

I volunteered for the service, though – Kasey is one of the few authors I have solicited to work with. What can I say? I'm a sucker for a woman writer, especially one with drive and focus. I can't afford a therapist so I choose to surround myself with goal-oriented, positive people... who write spine-numbing, nail-shredding horror in their spare time.

What I discovered, after meeting Kasey a few times and exchanging a few dozen emails, is that—like me—Kasey is afraid of everything. She says, quite simply, "I write about what scares me." We connected on an intrinsic level because we both grew up in Bible-centric homes. This affects your outlook; it affects your fears and your reactions to those fears. There's sin, and fear, and loss... and fear, and not being able to wake up because the nightmare is real.

The process of editing and revising this book for publication was an organic and very special experience for me, and I think Kasey would agree. Working on *Pieces of Madness* together, something happened beyond the page: we became friends through Microsoft Word comments and email exchanges.

Kasey not only welcomed me into her stories, she allowed me, and helped me, to dissect and splice and embellish in order to better communicate her vision. Kasey birthed these stories; I was her midwife. (Too much? I don't think so. There's an intimacy to word exchange too often underestimated.)

When we tap into the depths and precision of language we see the roots of human civilization, and when those words deal with primal fears and paranoia, we touch something deeply embedded in human culture.

There was certainly something intensely female in our exchange, particularly at first where there was a lot of buffering and politely hedging our points: "Is it okay that I did this?" "Oh, I'm so embarrassed that I made that mistake." My personal favorite is when I channeled Alfred from *Batman*: "Do let me know if you make further changes so I can review them."

Eventually the kid-gloves came off and we became a power couple, researching ideas, citing sources, disemboweling a passage and rewriting it from scratch. Our polite email and comment exchange turned into full-on discussions of Protestant and Catholic theology, the biblical roots of original sin, Oliver Sachs, and whether the criminally insane have souls, lessons in anatomy and taxidermy, the behavior of blood and lessons in blood spatter and rigor mortis ("How long after death does the body bruise and bloat?").

At one point, I offered to pay Kasey a dollar if she used a word in a story—it was a perfect fit. It's my dad's favorite word, and now when I read it I think of him: *Petrochor*. He never knew it was buried in there for him. (On a related note, Kasey, I just remembered that I owe you a dollar.)

There were times we did not agree. When she stuck

to her guns about the ending of "Bestia," I backed off. These are her stories, not mine. And of course, she was right. She also didn't take my advice when I compared the sound of mucous to "cooked pasta." (Before you write me off as a failure in everything that I do, I didn't actually suggest that. I was merely trying to get more out of the description and threw the "cooked pasta" reference out there. It worked. Kasey wrote a helluva creepy, disgusting scene—sans carbs, of course.) I did, however, manage to convince her to soften the moment when the principal speaks to the children about the death of the Mallerd boy in "Luke"—in the original version, he showed up like a drill sergeant and threatened to "pink slip" any of those eight-year-olds who stepped out of line. It was hilariously horrifying, but not completely necessary.

What was there, what I could not touch with line edits or replacing a comma, was the characters Kasey gives us. Her dialogue.

Kasey watches people. She studies them. This is evident in the ways her characters speak and the way they navigate their world.

Nowhere is this more apparent than in "His Majesty" where, you might have noticed, we completely eschewed dialogue rules. My editor comrades and grammar sticklers everywhere may have cringed, but the words needed to stand out on the page. Since Kasey and I were working together, I felt bold enough to exploit the rules, bend the practice. The layout of the words on the page was a deliberate choice to reflect Linda's fractured psyche. If this woman can break with sanity enough to peel the corpse of her husband, layer by layer, I thought it fitting that her thoughts and dialogue appear on the page as some sort of psychotic, taxidermic poetry.

The stories in this collection represent the manifest darkness in all of us. Some of these fears are within us, just a part of the author's imagination and upbringing; "Bestia" and "Sins of the Father" are clear reflections of that. On the other hand, the fear of a real monster, or real loss, shapes us as well, and forms the basis for "His Majesty." That story was inspired by Kasey's fears while her mother battled cancer. "Dollface" was especially disconcerting for me because, even after reading it about twelve times through, I'm still not sure if the Doctor is really a doctor, or if he's been a patient there the whole time. Uncertainty like that is, well... maddening.

The stories Kasey wrote for the second edition only deepen the cloying uncertainty. "Steiner and Holmes," a sequel, of sorts, to "Sins of the Father," turns Satan into something out of *A Clockwork Orange*, and makes us question, yet again, if we're dealing with insanity or just pure evil. "Cara Mia," on the other hand, an Outsiders-gone-wrong "whodunit" tale with a Motown soundtrack, skirts the line between true love and insanity.

Again and again, Kasey leaves us chasing our tails, spinning around in a circle wondering which end is up and, more importantly, how the hell to get out and get far away. One last thing, though: Kasey has more up her sleeve. I've seen it. If there's an author to watch, you better believe it's Kasey Pierce.

Leah Lederman is a freelance writer and editor from the Indianapolis area, where she lives with her husband and two small boys, their dog and two cats. Since obtaining her Master's degree in English Literature in 2009, she's busied herself with writing, editing, parenting, and teaching (though not always in that order). She started her own parenting column in "The Toledo Free Press", and has had her short stories published by "Bloodlotus", "Online Literary Journal", the Indianapolis Indie magazine "Snacks", the anthology *"A Matter of Words"*, and most recently in *"Issues of Tomorrow: A Sci-fi Anthology"*. *(Several other pieces are awaiting rejection.)* As an editor, she's worked with several indie comic authors, including Dirk Manning, Howie Noel, and *"Headmetal Comics"*. She has been featured on the comics news sites *"Creator Owned Expo"* and *"The Outhousers."* In addition, Leah has edited short story collections, children's books, a dissertation, and several novels.

ABOUT THE AUTHOR

Kasey Pierce is a horror/sci-fi author from the Metro Detroit area. Currently, she's written sci-fi comic series, "Norah" for Source Point Press. Other credits include the foreword for Gothic werewolf novella, "Rampant" (*Joshua Werner*) and the afterword for morbid-satire comic, "Dead Duck and Zombie Chick: Rising From the Grave". (*Jay Fosgitt*). She's also the author of John Marroquin's upcoming sci-fi graphic novel, "Mexica". (2017) Currently, she's working on an action-drama with writer, Bob Salley and has a part in an undisclosed project with *Rocket Ink Studios*.

To find out more, visit kosmickasey.com.